I0604283

Appointment with the Unknown:
The Hotel Stories

Evelyn Klebert

Appointment with the Unknown:
The Hotel Stories
By Evelyn Klebert

A Cornerstone Book
Published by Cornerstone Book Publishers
Copyright © 2020 & 2023 by Evelyn Klebert

All rights reserved under International and Pan-American Copyright Conventions. No part of this book may be reproduced in any manner without permission in writing from the copyright holder, except by a reviewer, who may quote brief passages in a review.

Cover Art and Interior Photographs by E.D. Poll

Cornerstone Book Publishers
Hot Springs Village, AR
www.cornerstonepublishers.com

First Cornerstone Edition – 2020
Second Cornerstone Edition – 2023

"I find the lure of the unknown irresistible."

Sylvia Earle

Dedication:

For Dana

Table of Contents

Appointment with the Unknown:
The Hotel Stories

Too Many Pens

She had too many pens — pens that wrote smoothly, pens that hesitated and jolted in her hands, pens that felt like pencils hitting the paper roughly and producing lovely, jagged lines. And then there were the ones that had almost run out, fading in and out on the paper — sometimes conducive to scribbling to jar them back to life.

Really, she supposed, she should throw at least some of them away. All they amounted to was clutter filling up her purse — scattered in the dark abyss of her bag. But she didn't let them go and could not reasonably articulate why. She would like to think that she was someone who didn't give up on things — people, for instance.

What a romantic notion, but of course, it wasn't true at all. She'd given up on plenty of things — jobs, places to live, and, yes, people. There was a smattering of incongruent relationships left on the trash heap, and family as well, a brother and sister she never spoke to.

She frowned, feeling dissatisfied. Perhaps, that was the core of things. She was profoundly dissatisfied.

She glanced down at the vibrantly blue carpet in the hotel room as a small black cairn terrier scuttled around one corner of the double-size bed. It wasn't amongst the echelon of exceptional hotels — La Hacienda — but they did take pets for no charge and bragged of a complimentary continental breakfast. All of this perfectly fit the bill for an out-of-work commercial artist. Of course, the word commercial chafed her artistic soul. She had never wanted to be a commercial anything. While, in most quarters, it equated to monetary reward, it always rang a bit of selling out. She'd always envisioned herself as purely an artist, no commercialism attached.

"Is there a spoon for the cereal?"

"I'm not allowed to put out everything until after 7 AM."

She frowned, pulling her cell phone from her pocket. "It is seven."

The hawkish-looking woman with thin red hair noticeably grimaced, then disappeared into a nearby doorway.

She put down the small Styrofoam bowl rejecting the compulsion to reach into the glass cereal container with her hand. Instead, she opted for juice, pressing a button that, yes, undeniably, was not working.

Free indeed, well you get what you pay for.

She moved to one of the small tables in the side room connected to the hotel lobby. Of course, she wasn't the only one waiting for the much sought-after continental breakfast. A few tables over, an unremarkable man sat reading a newspaper, wearing a dark-framed pair of glasses. She looked away, wishing she'd brought something to read so she didn't look as if she were waiting — waiting for something that was purportedly free.

She glanced up as the wiry red-haired employee continued slowly bringing paraphernalia into the dining room — batter for the waffle maker, syrup, tongs — no spoon for the cereal.

"The juice doesn't work," she blurted out. Why exactly? No other reason than frustration bursting from her lips.

The waitress, for lack of a better description, glared back at her. God, how she must hate her job. "What?" She snapped in her general direction.

It was clear that free was too pricey for this. "I said the juice machine doesn't work. I tried it."

The woman continued to glare back at her a bit, or perhaps she didn't. Perhaps, it was just her perception. But as she perceived it, the disgruntled employee stopped at the juice machine, managed a few quick hidden manipulations that her body hid from view, then returned to her preoccupation with the waffle maker. "Should work now," she tossed out over a perceptively cold shoulder. Did her presence really merit all this grief? And then, she was gone again, vanishing through that mysterious door that, in retrospect, wasn't all that mysterious — a back storeroom of some sort, no doubt containing a spoon large enough to serve the breakfast cereal.

"Someone's having a bad day."

She glanced quickly across several tables to meet the eyes of the nondescript man. He'd taken off the reading glasses. "I meant her, not you," he commented dryly.

"Feels like she's trying to make me have a bad day," she muttered, nearly under her breath.

Eyes, eyes that were brown — maybe hazel. "Well, best not to let that happen. You can get your juice now."

She stood up, not really smiling but feeling slightly better. "Small favors."

"All we can ask for," he murmured, returning to his paper.

What qualified as a remarkable man? To the artist, or at least to her forty-eight-year-old ever so slightly jaundiced artist eye, something of interest in the face. Sculpted bone structure, prominent eyes, perhaps an unusual scar or incongruity of features — a mouth too full, too sensual, or something that shatters the unexpected. At least for her, this was the case.

Next time she would bring something to occupy her — her sketchbook, although she couldn't imagine anything of note that she'd want to sketch here.

There was nothing of interest, nothing of intensity, of violent beauty.

After her cereal and juice, she grabbed a small banana nut muffin in a napkin to bring to Audriana upstairs. The man, the original one, because a few other early-morning eaters had drifted in, remained engrossed in his paper.

There was a cup and an empty plate in front of him. She hadn't noticed when he had eaten. She hadn't noticed, so she threw out her trash and headed through the lobby back to the elevators.

They called her Rayne, Rayne Peters. Or rather, at some point, she'd started calling herself that. The family had always called her Rayna, oddly named for some android woman from an old Star Trek episode — the original series, not the newer ones. Her mother, or perhaps it was her father, was a fan.

Yes, it was unique, and her derivation of it afforded a nice, memorable script to etch on her creations — unless they were for a company, a contracted work, designed in Photoshop or Illustrator. Those paid the bills — though she wasn't allowed to put much of a personal imprint on them.

They were on the third floor — she and Audriana. She had an interview in town tomorrow morning. The hotel she was in was on the city's outskirts, which suited her just fine. It was amidst a little cluster of gas stations, a Cracker Barrel, and convenience shops.

She'd arrived last night, no, the night before. She'd wanted a little time to prepare herself. How she despised changing jobs — having to remake or rather sell herself to a new employer. It had been some years since she had to do so, definitely not in practice. In fact, it felt like parts of her mind, her body, had somewhat atrophied to the point that she needed to reawaken them to accomplish the task. But in the corner of the room was quite a substantial artist's portfolio — a well-put-together representation of her work. So, there was no reason not to feel confident.

She laid back on the bed and closed her eyes. Audriana snuggled her hand momentarily, then moved away. It was the fatigue she carried that was the worst of it, mostly in her chest. She should get it checked out, but she didn't really want to — didn't want to deal with much of anything.

And there was something about the second floor. At first, she thought it just might be that hideous carpet, purple with odd beige and green spirals that reminded her of garish octopus tentacles. But, of course, it was the same hallway carpet they used on all the floors.

"Enjoying your stay here?" He'd snuck up on her. Exactly how that had happened, she had no idea. She was sitting or rather lounging out by the pool, not really in a swimsuit, though she had one underneath, but just a pair of white shorts and a gray T-shirt from a long-ago Florida vacation. She glanced up from beneath her floppy blue straw hat into the eyes of that unremarkable man. He had a beard and mustache. That hadn't really registered before. "Sorry, what did you say?"

"I asked if you are enjoying your time here."

"Oh," she said. What a peculiar thing to ask. "I'm here on business. That's why I'm here," she murmured.

He sat in a lounge chair beside hers and held out his hand. "Thomas Ward."

She took his hand in hers, firm grip, warm grip. "Rayne, Rayne Peters."

He was smiling, dark hair with gray here and there. "So, then you're not enjoying your stay," he said with humor in his voice. Was he flirting with her? It had been so long. She had no idea. He was probably late forties, early fifties — around her age. Could be flirting.

"It's just a hotel, nothing special."

He nodded, "Well, I'll be here a few days. In case, you need a friendly face." He stood up. He was leaving as abruptly as he'd arrived.

"Are you on the second floor?" She blurted out.

He looked at her a bit oddly. "No, I'm on the third."

She nodded. She should've told him she was as well, but she was preserving her solitude. After all, she wouldn't be here long.

The elevator had stopped and opened on the second floor. She hadn't been paying attention, so that was why she stepped out, not recognizing the fact until the doors speedily swished closed behind her.

Of course, it looked like the third floor, but those shiny oval metal discs on the off-white doors all denoted numbering in the two hundreds.

Of course, she thought to turn around and press the button again to summon the elevator, but she didn't. She just stood there — eyes drawn to the ugly purple carpet with its tentacle-like effigies and the dim lights down the long narrow hallway.

After every set of three rooms, there was a squarish light fixture, a clear box mounted on the wall. She decided to take the stairs. After all, it was only one floor.

But she didn't move, oddly felt compulsively rooted, almost dizzy. It was hotter here, like a wave of heat from the carpet rising. She forced herself to turn and push the heavy door leading to the stairway, quickly ascending the cold stone steps as if something was nipping at her heels.

The next morning, she waited until 7:15 AM for breakfast. As expected, the red-haired server, waitress, perhaps barista, was slowly setting up the counter. Thomas, Thomas Ward, was sitting at his same table with a newspaper. He glanced up casually, smiled briefly, then returned to his reading.

She started with a cup of coffee, headed to a nearby table, but then hesitated, caught by spontaneity. Stepping closer to him, she said awkwardly, "So, are you enjoying your stay?" Her voice was low and choppy feeling, as though she had not used it in some time.

He looked at her speculatively. "Would you like to join me for breakfast?" He had warm eyes. And she was so tired of thinking about herself.

She sipped her coffee, which had a discernible burnt flavor underneath. Of course, why they were serving burnt coffee first thing in the morning was beyond her.

"Why did you think I was on the second floor?"

"Oh, I guess that was strange. It just popped into my head. I ended up there the other day, accidentally. I'm on the third."

"Which number?"

She hated when she ended up in a corner, feeling compelled to give out information. So many times in her life, people had done just that — cornered her. If she didn't give them what they wanted, she seemed rude. If she did, she felt she'd given something away that she didn't want to.

"You don't have to tell me," he said, closing off that particular discussion in her mind.

She sipped the burnt coffee again. She'd opted for cereal and yogurt today — blueberry, although she preferred strawberry, which was unavailable.

"So, you're alone here?"

She glanced up, yes definitely warm eyes, and an interesting face, a bit tanned. He really wasn't as nondescript as she'd originally thought. He was subtle, and she had not taken the time to notice that initially.

"Well, not completely. I have a dog — a small cairn terrier, Audriana."

He smiled, "Pretty name."

"Yes, well, she's skittish. Are you — I mean on your own?" It felt safe to echo questions he'd already broached. So, it wasn't as though she was encroaching on new territory.

"Yes," was all he said.

"Do you like swimming?"

"Oh, I don't know. It's been so long since I've done it."

"But you brought a suit."

Did she? Her mind felt oddly clouded today. She'd run into Thomas Ward downstairs at the vending machines. There was a small alcove next to the lobby filled with the requisite sodas, chips, and, surprisingly enough, a machine filled with ice cream treats that she had yet to sample.

"Yes, I did bring one." The vision of a black utilitarian-type suit built for middle-aged women popped into her mind.

He had a beige sports jacket on today over a vibrant blue shirt. He really did not look nondescript at all today but instead somewhat fetching. He put one hand on the soda machine, leaning casually. "So, bringing a swimsuit does indicate some intent."

She looked up at him, scrutinizing a bit. "Mr. Ward, Thomas, I don't know what you have in mind, but I won't be here very long."

"Just company, maybe some interesting conversation."

She smiled, undeniably a bit drawn in. It felt good to have attention again. "And swimming?"

"It very well might involve swimming."

She didn't know anything about him. And he hadn't really asked anything about her. She'd always defined herself by what she did. She was an artist. She was a commercial artist. She was a website artist. The list of variations stretched on and on. But none of that had been spoken of. Once she got Audriana settled in and fed, she dressed in her utilitarian black bathing suit, pulled a t-shirt over it, and pulled on a pair of white denim shorts.

Vaguely, she acknowledged that she'd skipped lunch, but it wasn't unusual. When she slid her room key into the lock on the black gate at the pool, she saw that Thomas was already in the water. She headed to a nearby table, putting down one of the room towels she'd brought.

"Water is great. Come in," he beckoned.

She smiled. As it was, they were alone, which was just as well. She'd intended to leave on the t-shirt, but there he was, no shirt, just swim trunks. If she did, he'd probably think she was some kind of a prude, all covered up. So, she took off the shirt and shorts, then sat on the edge of the pool near the steps, feet, and legs dangling in the water.

He eased up to her and sat beside her, smiling warmly. "Aren't you coming in, Rayne?"

"Trying to adjust feels a little chilly to me."

"Only at first, princess, then you acclimate."

"Well, I've never been a great acclimator."

He continued smiling. "I can see that about you. Why don't you come in anyway?"

And then he took her hand and began tugging at her. "I don't like to be pushed."

"I'm not pushing. I'm coaxing."

Her feet sort of fumbled down the steps as she followed his lead. The water hit her in an icy rush. "Damn," it just came out.

"Give it a second." Now they were standing, standing well past the steps as the water sloshed up coolly around her neck and shoulders.

"Maybe I'm just getting numb."

"Numb has its advantages." He was still holding her hands, both just in front of her.

"You know this isn't really like me."

Another smile, "That's okay."

Water, cool water enveloped her — her heart, her skin. It lowered the temperature of things, and she breathed in deeply.

"Isn't this better?"

The sky overhead was cloudy, breaking the oppressive heat of the summer day. "It could storm."

"That's okay." He hadn't let go of her hands, just continued to lead her deeper into the pool. But how deep did it go? She was five feet, five inches. She glanced at its curved side. Five feet seemed to be the limit.

Looking back at him, she could see how intensely he was watching her. "I've got you. Don't worry."

Then he pulled her closer and placed her hands on his shoulders. She didn't know his intent. He must be making a pass — trying to pull her in. But it felt different somehow, undeniably.

Of course, she'd had lovers before, boyfriends early on, even a potential fiancé — and of course, the other kind of lovers with the understanding that this was all it would be. Then, it had been just her, alone, for some time.

He stopped in the middle of the pool, not really near the walls but nearer the deep end. Her hands remained on his shoulders, muscular solid, dark wet hair matting his chest mingled with gray. When she'd begun to see the gray sprinkling her chestnut-colored hair, she wondered if that was signaling the end of things for her. Then she'd colored them and made them disappear.

His hand slipped onto her waist, and he pulled her even closer. "You know. I know nothing at all about you," she murmured.

"You're very beautiful, Rayne," he said softly before he kissed her.

His lips were warm, soft, inviting, and reminding her of comfort.

Audriana was quiet, content to lay in the other double-size bed as she and Thomas Ward made love in her hotel room. She didn't need birth control. Menopause had hit her at forty-three, so the possibility of children slipped away silently and noticeably at that point.

"You could always adopt. Single women do that all the time."

"Single women who are wealthy," had been her reply. There was a cost to pursuing her muse. It didn't provide much of an income.

She'd hung their damp swimsuits across the bathroom shower curtain bar and given him a towel to dry off with before they'd gotten into bed.

She'd had lovers before, but she felt nervous with this man who held her in a way that felt curiously as though it was his whole goal to comfort her. And it still felt intense but soft, as though being gentle with her was his entire purpose. And then after, he'd just continue to hold her tightly.

"I don't even know what you do."

"I'm a teacher," he said softly, kissing the top of her head. She didn't know why she had done this. Traditionally, she didn't just jump into bed with a man. But it had all felt so good, his hands, his embrace, his body next to hers, on top of hers. It felt like a sweet soft drug calming her.

"At a university?"

"Something like that."

She sat up, pulling the bed sheets up with her. "You really don't want to give me any information, do you?"

He smiled, softly touching her arm. "I enjoy living in the moment."

"Because there isn't going to be any future?"

He sighed, pulling her down insistently but softly. "You need to let go, Rayne. Stop worrying so much."

Then his insistent mouth was on hers, and it did help to put her in that dreaming place where her thoughts drifted away.

When she woke up, it was nighttime, and he was gone. She felt so heavily groggy that she was dizzy when she stood up. She flicked on the lights in the bathroom and saw that only her swimsuit was hanging there now. Looking in the mirror, she was a bit surprised. Her shoulder-length hair, though in disarray, was nearly dry, and her normally pale cheeks looked flushed.

And then the phone rang, making her jump because it wasn't her cell phone. which had a musical tone. This was a hard, jarring ring. She moved out of the bedroom, still feeling disoriented, and spotting instead the phone on the desk in the corner of the room that, quite frankly, she hadn't taken note of before.

She sank into the black faux leather and metal desk chair and picked up the heavy receiver. "Hello."

"Rayne," it was him, that soft but deep masculine voice.

"Yes."

"I didn't want to wake you earlier when I left, but I needed to change into some dry clothes. How about you come to my place for dinner tonight? About half an hour."

"Your place?"

He laughed, "Down the hall, room 326."

"Oh, yeah, well, okay."

"I'll see you then."

"Okay," and then she hung up. Her heart was slamming in her chest a bit. What in the world was she getting into?

She wore a short sleeve black hooded sweater over a pair of white shorts, pulling her shoulder-length hair back into a messy bun. With it, she put on a long silver chain with a silver locket shaped like a heart. It had been a gift long ago. Her mother, she thought. And the earrings were silver dangling leaves with garnets woven in.

So, this was a peculiar date of sorts. She'd tucked her room key into one pocket of her shorts and then headed down the hallway.

The carpet was the same as on the second floor, that curious purplish green-beige montage that stretched into clumsy swirls. But oddly, on the second floor, it had looked worse, more menacing. She could easily bring the pattern up in her mind with its huge, convoluted tentacles.

She deliberately pushed the creepy images aside as she stopped in front of his door — Thomas's, number 326.

Taking a quick, determined breath, she lightly tapped. Within seconds, the door opened, and he greeted her with a warm smile. "I hope you like pizza."

Pizza and white wine, Pinot Grigio. "Shouldn't it be red?" She asked lightly.

They were sitting on either side of the desk, exactly like the one in her room. Where he managed to produce two plastic wine glasses, she had no idea, except she suspected some convenience store nearby.

The pizza was recognizable — Dominos Supreme or something of the like. "So, did you rest any?" he inquired, watching her closely. The real question, she supposed, was did you get any rest after making passionate love to a stranger in her hotel bed?

"Yes, a little," she said. And then he squeezed her hand. Warm, druggy sensations flooded through her skin.

"You need to relax," he said lightly, running his fingertips across the top of her hand. Just that light touch seemed to melt away so much tension that she had been carrying.

"I am. I mean, I think I am," she said. And then he pulled her up to her feet and again pulled her into an embrace. She didn't know him, but he felt curiously familiar and oh so comfortable. Before he began to kiss her again, she said softly, "What about dinner?"

"We have a microwave," then the rapid swirl of passion and the sensation of letting go.

She slept for a while. She was certain of it. At times, Thomas seemed beside her and then not at others. The sheets had a crispy, freshly laundered feel soothing against her skin. And then, there was also the comforter, blue satin, not like the off-white and black swirl pattern that had been on her bed, not like the one that had been on the king-size bed in his hotel room.

Her eyes flickered open, and sunlight spilled across the room that she didn't recognize.

Across from the bed was a white wicker chair, other creamy-colored furniture, and at one end of the room, a set of open French doors. Her head spun with the delicious dizziness that made her feel as though she was somewhat inebriated. But that white wine, she had taken very little of it.

She was naked beneath the white sheets, but oddly she didn't remember much, just kissing, intense, passionate kisses.

And then he walked inside through the French doors, smiling, dressed in a long beige cable sweater over khaki pants. "It's a little chilly out. You might need a robe."

She glanced around again with confusion. "It's August. Why would it be cold?"

He sat on the side of the bed, capturing her hand. "February, my dear, even on the beach, it gets chilly in February."

She sat up, things flipping over strangely in her mind. She remembered the hotel, the ugly purple carpet, Audriana. Her eyes widened, Audriana. She'd forgotten entirely about Audriana.

He put his hand on her arm. "It's all right," he said.

And then she woke up in a hotel room. She glanced over. Thomas was asleep, the wine and pizza virtually untouched on the desk.

She felt him shift beside her, then his hands on her beneath the sheets. "I need to go," she said with a little agitation. "I have a dog. I forgot to feed her."

"It's all right. We'll bring her some pizza. I'll go with you," he said, lightly kissing her.

When she first slipped the key card into the lock and opened the hotel room door, she'd forgotten about why they were there. Thomas had brought what remained of the pizza, including some crust pieces in the pizza box. She felt so light in his company, happy, she supposed, and in some ways thoroughly distracted.

Once they'd entered the room, he placed the box on the desk and pulled her into his arms to kiss her. "I'd like to take you to the coast, near the beach."

The vividness of that dream came into sharp relief. What had he said? "Even on the beach, it gets chilly in February," she murmured aloud.

He pulled back a bit, "Yes, I prefer the coast in the winter."

Why was she here? Glancing around in a strange sort of disorientation, she canvassed the room's floor — then she remembered. It took a few moments, but finally, she saw the dark shape poke her head around the corner of the bed closest to the window.

She felt a strange sort of relief because for a moment, just for a moment, she felt afraid that she wouldn't see her at all.

He sat on the bed and gently patted the little black dog's head. "And is this Audriana?" he asked.

"Yes," she murmured, "I have a meeting tomorrow, an interview in town," she said in a sort of vague tone. She felt as though she was losing track of things somehow, and she needed to solidify what was important or it —

"Do you want me to give her the crusts?"

"Crusts?"

"Pizza crusts."

"Oh yes, that's right."

He smiled at her with no reflection of the strangeness she was feeling. Sitting quietly on the bed, she watched him feed the little dog. "Have you been on the second floor?" she asked for no real reason except that it popped into her head.

"Yes," he said quietly.

"It's cold there," she replied.

"Then maybe you should avoid it."

She thought perhaps he was married. But there was no evidence of a wedding ring. She thought he probably would leave in a few days, but he didn't mention doing so. She needed context to understand this affair if that was what it was. Perhaps a fling — but he had done nothing to indicate that he was not fully engaged in what was happening between them.

He'd spent the night in her room. He managed to get a small plate of tuna for Audriana from a nearby store. And he stayed the night. They hadn't really discussed it.

It felt soothing to her to be held by him. She couldn't compare it to any former relationships or involvements she'd had. It was, in some respects, too easy, too natural. They existed in some sort of cocoon, an uncomplicated state of being.

And she began to relax.

The next day they went out and walked a great deal. They took Audriana with them and later went out by themselves again.

It should've been hotter than it was. The weather actually felt quite temperate.

"What is your home like?"

"It's lovely. I have a place by the water. I like to sail."

"I've never been sailing."

"I could take you if you like." That certainly didn't sound as though he was married.

"I really hate the carpet on the second floor."

"On the second floor?" he repeated.

"Yes, it's so ugly, purples and those awful swirls that look like tentacles. Have you seen it?"

"I suppose," he murmured.

"I mean, I guess it's the same carpet on the other floors, but it seems different there."

He squeezed her hand. "Are you happy, Rayne?"

"Well, I suppose," she said a bit vaguely.

"You know. It's all right to let yourself be."

They had coffee downstairs in the lobby the following day. They let themselves dawdle so much that they nearly missed it.

The red-haired attendant was there, but she seemed nicer and somehow softened a bit now that she was with Thomas. Then again, maybe she just didn't care as much about how other people were acting or what they were doing.

She smiled at him, "Is the breakfast getting better here, or am I just imagining it?"

He squeezed her hand. They were holding hands a lot. They were sitting at one of the small tables in the breakfast area, and he was holding her hand that was resting on the middle of the table. It didn't really make sense that he was married because he certainly wasn't trying to hide their involvement. He was affectionate, holding her hand, putting his arm around her, and even stopping, and kissing her in public.

But it was true. Things were improving around here — biscuits for breakfast, bacon, scrambled eggs, fresh coffee.

Again, he squeezed her hand. "I was thinking I'd like to take you somewhere else."

She smiled, distracted by his lovely enthusiasm. Maybe she wasn't really a dalliance, but even so, men did take their mistresses on trips. "I don't know."

"I have a beach house. I think you'd like it."

The dream rushed up again in her mind. It didn't make sense at all that she'd dream about a place first, then hear about it later. "You know. I have things I need to get back to."

It was vague in her mind again why she was here. Who she was. But it was strong, the image of that airy room, a satin comforter, French doors leading outside.

"Don't push so hard," he said.

It was confusing. What did that mean? After breakfast, they entered the elevator. It was patterned with a curious gold leaf-looking metal on its doors. As it began to move up, she abruptly pushed the button for the second floor.

"Why did you do that?" he asked.

"I wanted to see it again."

He didn't comment, just looked forward. Was he angry? Didn't seem so. Disapproving? Why should he be? It was only another floor of the hotel. The elevator sort of lurched a bit as it landed on the second floor. "I'd hoped —" Then he stopped.

What could it be that he'd hoped?

"Rayne, are you still on your own?"

"Why don't you come home?"

"Why don't you stay in touch with someone?"

The light seemed to flicker in the hallway. She stepped out of the elevator, and he followed only moments later. It seemed some time before the doors closed behind them. Cosmetically, it was designed much the same as the third floor, but then the lights flickered again, all of them at once, on and off, from brightness to shadows.

"Why does it feel so different here?"

"It's a different level. That's all."

Different level. Didn't he mean to say different floor? She moved forward, and the air felt thicker somehow, warm but dense as well. Maybe it was some strange sort of chemicals they were using to clean with, or maybe they'd just painted. But the walls didn't look freshly painted. On the contrary, they seemed a bit worn.

She moved on ahead but slowly. "What are you hoping to find?" he asked, just behind her.

"Find? What would I find here? It's just another floor of the hotel."

"I was hoping you'd let me take you away."

She glanced down at the ugly purple carpet with its strange swirls of green and brown and yellow too. Not a pretty yellow like she would've used in her paintings — warm and gold like the sun, but an ugly flat, dark yellow, not inspired.

"I was giving you time. You know," he said.

It was like coiling, coiling serpents around her feet, reaching up to her ankles. That was what this carpet seemed to her. How could anyone bear to be on this floor? How could they sleep, rest? She stopped, everything swirling now. There was a key in her hand, a keycard that she didn't remember having. She held it up, examining it with curiosity. It said 217, room 217.

"Why do I have this?"

"You've always tended to dwell in dark places."

"I—" then she hesitated.

She had checked into the hotel. She remembered that, but the key they'd given her was this one, not the other. "I don't understand," she murmured.

"It was difficult."

She abruptly swiped the key in the lock, room 217. Inside was dimly lit, and it smelled, almost a stink of some sort, and it was warm. She checked the thermostat. It was on 85. "Why is it so hot?"

"The occupant was confused. They felt so cold."

She walked in toward the far bed near the window. Someone was lying there, and it was rank. It had been days.

"It might be better to leave now." She felt his hand on her arm. She remembered it, remembered the chill, couldn't get warm.

"I — who is that who —"

He pulled her gently out of the room into the hallway, closing the door behind them. "It was some sort of stroke," he said. "Happened quickly."

"Thomas—"

He was holding her hand. "We're going to leave now. We can talk about things later. I'll take you to the beach house for a while, and you can rest. Audriana is already there, waiting for you."

She didn't ask him how that was possible. But she could remember losing the little black dog many years ago when she was a girl. They waited for the elevator, holding hands, and she relaxed. Whatever was coming next, would no doubt be extraordinary.

Slipping

She'd checked into a hotel off of US Highway 65. It was on the outskirts of somewhere, some town or city, heading into the Ozarks. She hadn't paid much attention, just stopped when things started becoming unbearable.

"Just one?" The girl at the receptionist's desk had asked—just *one*, as though it were an oddity. The world was filled with people who were *Just One*, traveling this great canvas all by themselves. But she didn't belabor the point. She was deeply in need of a shower and a soft pillow to rest her weary mind upon.

"Enjoy your stay, Ms. Ascher."

She was not married, thirty-four and more single, she thought, than most people.

She took the elevator up to the third floor. Her surroundings were not penetrating her psyche just now. It took every effort to reach her destination down a long, insufficiently lit hallway. But perhaps it wasn't the lighting, perhaps just her eyes not functioning properly.

She slid in the card, opening the doorway to room 302. She let the heavy door close behind her, plopping her large shoulder-carrying bag onto one of the two double beds. The room was large, beige, decorated sparsely with a few oversized floral photographs. The beds were unremarkable, with white bedspreads and dark burgundy, cotton bed skirts. The headboards were a dark wood of a cheap variety, as was the rest of the furniture. As hotels went, it was serviceable, and her skin wasn't crawling.

She pulled her long black hair out of its ponytail and shook it out. Even in her thoughts, that sounded, well, snobby. But it wasn't actually. It was literal.

Many places felt simply, physically intolerable to her. She laid back on one of the beds and closed her eyes. She was so tired. With distraction, she wondered why they gave her two beds if she was *Just One.*

She heard the fly buzzing around her, and her eyes flickered open. A chill of recognition traveled up her spine. Evidently, she was not *Just One.* There was something else here with her.

He must have been only half an hour behind her. It was eight in the evening when he pulled into the Ozark Mountain Motel. It was late afternoon when he first learned that a traveler was passing through the area. He was just leaving his office when the first wave hit him. It felt a bit like a strong current of erratic weather rushing through the landscape, a sudden storm but not a focused one, though evidently only apparent to those tuned in. Immediately, he'd cleared his mind, sending out feelers to his network.

"What is it?"

More like someone.

"Are you sure? It doesn't feel like anything I've ever sensed before."

Yes, the consensus is it's a traveler.

"A traveler, you mean a time traveler?"

No, no different, maybe dimensional.

Now that had given him pause, he'd been studying esotericism and parapsychology for nearly twenty-plus years, and he'd never encountered a dimensional traveler.

Do you want me to follow it up? There seems to be something wrong there.

"No," he'd sent out almost involuntarily. *"Let me. I've never encountered anyone capable of dimensional travel before."*

At this point, it really isn't clear what she's capable of.

"She?" He'd asked, surprised, but why exactly he wasn't clear. He'd just assumed it was a man. Perhaps that was a tinge chauvinistic of him.

Yes, late twenties, early thirties it seems. But the energy is erratic. Be careful.

"Yes," he'd answered, getting in his car. There was an overnight bag in the trunk already packed in case, well, just in case, the unexpected might happen. And this, as much as anything, qualified as unexpected.

It seemed like a dream at first. No, that wasn't true. It seemed like a nightmare, a waking nightmare. Nina woke up in her bed, and she had slipped, though at the time she didn't know it. Where she found herself was dark, shadowy, but undeniably her bedroom. She remembered the horrible panicked feeling, her heart pounding wildly. She was only twelve. That's when it really started. Her menstrual cycle had just begun the week before, and it brought with it changes, clearly unforeseen changes to her psyche. Her mother had told her to be aware, cognizant of unexpected feelings, but she hadn't warned her about this.

She'd sat up in the bed, calling out, "Hello," but no answer. In fact just an eerie muffled sort of silence. Silence, until, of course, it wasn't. The movement began quickly, first in the shadowy corners of her room. There were things unseen there, things rustling, scurrying.

Cold fear energized her as she jumped out of bed and began running through the house. But it wasn't the house she knew. Everything was different, even the air, cumbersome, as though she was pushing through sand, heavy wet, mushy sand that clung to her skin, weighing her down and impeding movement. "Momma," she screamed in terror, but the sound of her voice was constricted, stifled in the thick darkness.

With Herculean effort, she moved from room to room, only to find each empty, filled with dense shadows. No one was there, yet it seemed they almost were. She could feel the heat in places, the heat of living bodies, the heaviness of form that was simply not quite where it should be. Again, she opened her mouth to scream, but it was as though she was swallowing the murky atmosphere around her, thick in her lungs. There was no doubt in her mind that this would kill her if she remained. She was literally drowning in this place.

And then, joltingly, she was back, as though she'd just awoken from a bad dream. But it didn't feel like a dream because that place was still inside her, making her sick. She thrashed in her mother's arms. "Nina," she whispered in her hair. "It's all right. You're back home now," and it chilled her because it was clear that her mother knew exactly what had happened.

They called it slipping, her mother, her grandmother. But it was a secret, something not spoken of — a curse of sorts, they believed, passed from daughter to daughter. It bypassed the men, her uncles, her brother, being immune and completely ignorant of it.

"Shouldn't we tell them?" she'd asked.

"They wouldn't understand," was their answer. "They will believe something is wrong with your mind."

"But I don't understand. What is that place?"

Her mother had remained silent, and then her grandmother had spoken. "It's another realm, a dark place, just next to us. A terrible place, I think. That was how my mother described it. There are things there that shouldn't be seen, shouldn't be known about. The best thing to do is to try to learn to keep yourself here and ignore it."

That was all that was said, their best advice, she surmised. And when she tried to speak of it again, she was stonewalled.

Usually, she was pretty successful in anchoring herself. Unless, well, unless she was too tired or run-down. Over the years, Nina became an expert in monitoring her physical and emotional state. And, of course, relationships were a problem. She started dating in college, Jerry. And then it became a battle, a constant struggle.

A year or so into their union, she'd spent the weekend with him and found herself trapped in the middle of the night in the cabin with things, horrible distorted things in those shadows. She'd concluded that there was an emotional component to all of this. The next day she had him take her home, and she broke up with him soon after. She would be *Just One*. Decidedly, it seemed the only solution.

She opened her eyes and watched the fly bounce off the hotel room's ceiling. It wasn't very big. But her instincts told her that it was much more than just a fly. Her eyes opened wider as it circled overhead. Louder, louder, the buzzing grew until she felt it in her fingertips, her hands, beneath her skin, then her blood synchronizing with the irritating pitch.

"Anchor yourself." She could hear her grandmother's voice from the past. But it was all too late. She noted as she slipped into the darkness.

He'd just begun to settle in his room on the third floor when he felt it. Something powerful seared through the energy around him. There was a distinct pull and pressure in his chest as he abruptly sat down on the hotel bed, trying to collect himself. Peter Lochlan breathed in deeply while focusing on centering himself again.

"She's traveling," he sent outward.

Yes, an answer. He was never really alone, just a directed thought away from obtaining much-needed guidance. *Are you sure you want to handle this?*

"Yes," though he didn't know why exactly, just something he felt strongly about. "She's *pulling energy.*"

It's not deliberate. It's done in a sort of panic.

"Do you think she's dangerous?"

It depends on what you mean by dangerous.

The room pulsated around her. It wasn't always the same. Where she ended up wasn't always the same. The hotel room wasn't couched in shadows but rather distorted, flickering light frequencies. And she could still hear that buzzing sound that the fly was making, but it was in everything, the walls, the furniture. The carpeted floor all pulsated at that strange reverberating pitch.

She moved rather fluidly back against the bed. This was the manner of movement here, a sort of liquid-like slithering, not unakin to swimming through jelly. She continued to stare at it. It was affixed to the pulsating ceiling. She should have screamed, but it was pointless. And she'd seen worse, much worse in her time. The fly had ballooned in size, its eyes glowing orange, all its eyes on its enormous head, now around the size of a small bear. Its legs fidgeted and pranced, moving around the ceiling as though trying hard to grasp its fluctuating surface. No, she was wrong. Perhaps, she should scream. It was zeroing in on her, undeniably positioning itself, wanting something.

She deliberately focused on the door, concentrating. Each place, each space, had its own rules. This place felt connected to it, to that thing. She didn't want to call it a fly because it wasn't really. That was only what it looked like in her world.

With will and concentration, she pushed off from the headboard, springing across the room to the door. When her hands made contact, she found the fluctuating wood thick and slimy. Wielding a fist through its unstable surface, then punching through, she pushed herself through the newly created opening, tumbling with significant force.

Again, she focused, being direct and mindful she'd learned were the tools of the trade in survival. The hallway was different, completely different, as though she'd passed into another level. Its ceiling was low and seemed to stretch endlessly, bending and curving out of her sight. Here, all the walls were a flickering, blinding white. She heard it behind her, scrambling, that horrible buzzing sound. The other place had been its domain, but it clearly was coming after her, hunting, predatory in nature.

She took off down the curving hall. But the more she traveled, the more it curved and bent like a confusing maze. She was stupid to have stopped here at this place, at the hotel, but she'd been so tired. This place was complicated, with so many pockets, unseen pockets. It would be easy to get lost.

Directly behind her, she heard it scuttling, that horrible, incessant buzzing noise. She could feel how it wanted to rip her to pieces in that pincer-like mouth. And if it did, would she be dead or just trapped somewhere unspeakable? Her calmness was deteriorating into panic. That could be deadly to her. She pushed forward, stumbling along the hallway's tight and uneven little walls. They went on and on relentlessly, with no place to break out of. And then she turned a sharp, sudden bend, and something or rather someone was standing there in front of her. Her vision was blurred here, but she clearly made out a form.

Her heart clutched in fear. In all the years she'd been doing this, experiencing these bizarre phenomena, she'd been alone, solitary, except for the ambient creatures. There was no one else. But this form, person she suspected, reached out toward her, jarringly grabbing her arm in a painful grip.

"Come on," she heard a voice inside her head and then felt an abrupt yank outward.

Nina sat up in the bed in her hotel room. She touched her face with the palms of her trembling hands — icy, sweaty, her heart cramping painfully in her chest. She physically jumped when the first knock came at her door and then the second, sharp, unrelenting. She looked around, still in that state of panic. She didn't see the fly. Perhaps, it had moved on. Then the third knock, just as fierce, reminded her sharply of the present. After that, it stopped for quite a space, nothing, just silence. If she waited, whoever it was might just leave. But there was something that began to pull at her, something powerful, insistent, drawing her to her feet.

Without thinking, without being able to stop herself, she reached out, opening the door.

A man was standing in the hallway, looking at her intently. "Are you all right?" he asked directly. And he reached out, catching her, as she began to collapse in exhaustion.

He had gotten her a glass of water and waited patiently as she took a sip. He watched her intensely as though every movement she made was of some peculiar fascination. "You need to leave this room. There's something in here that's not good."

She looked down into her clear glass of water, feeling intensely embarrassed. "It's a fly." She spoke softly. It was so awkward, so alien, speaking to anyone about this.

"A fly?"

"I mean, it looks like a fly, but I'm sure it's something else."

"Some sort of drainer?"

She frowned, looking up at him with some confusion. How could he know? Who was he? He wasn't an old man, maybe a bit older than her, but not terribly. He wore a long-sleeved white shirt, sleeves rolled up, and tan slacks. She wondered with distraction how it was possible that he was jumping into the middle of her secret world, and more than that, why. "Maybe," she murmured hesitantly.

"You're not the only one who knows things, sees the unseen, you know. There are many of us out there," he said quite solemnly.

"I—" she tried to speak, but it felt as though her breath had been cut by something.

"You're very tired. Get your things and come with me."

"Where?"

"My room, there aren't any flies there," he said flatly, though with just the hint of a smile.

Nina Ascher appeared oddly delicate to him — that long black hair she pulled up into a bun at the nape of her neck before they left and that pale porcelain-like complexion. Her skin felt cool, in fact, too cool and clammy as though she'd run a great distance. And as far as he could tell, she had indeed.

Peter was surprised that she seemed so willing to go with him. He hadn't expected, well, the truth was that he hadn't known what to expect. But he knew, as soon as he walked into her room, that there was something very problematic and even threatening there. He accepted her word that it was a fly. He'd seen odder things, and he was greatly concerned about her. Dimension traveler or not, she needed help.

As he opened the door to his hotel room, she slowly walked inside, a bit dazed. "What was your name again?" she nearly whispered.

"Peter, Peter Lochlan."

"Oh," he placed the overnight bag he'd taken from her room on the far bed. She glanced around tentatively with obvious distraction. "It looks like mine."

"No flies," he murmured, closing the door behind her. "Would you like a soda or something?"

"Maybe, but don't leave right now," she said hesitantly. "I'm so tired, worried I'll slip again."

"Slip?"

She laughed awkwardly. "That's what my grandmother used to call it, slipping."

"You mean dimension traveling?"

She looked at him with a bit of confusion. "Is that what I'm doing?"

"I think so."

She sat down gingerly on one of the beds. "Just don't leave. I feel so weak. If it happens again, I'm worried I won't come back."

It was calming being around him. She'd expected questions, but he was quiet. They'd walked down the hall largely in silence. He'd gotten her a Sprite from the vending machine and a Coke for himself. Then they'd returned to his room, a stranger's room she curiously felt safer in than her own.

"You must think I'm very peculiar," she commented as they made their way down the actually very unremarkable hallway.

"I think you're extraordinary," he answered softly.

That was shocking, comforting, having someone be so kind to her. The world she was used to was hard, and people were generally rough with her. He opened the door to his room, and she walked in but stopped just inside as the door closed behind them. She looked around, actually actively considering things for perhaps the first time since she'd met him. "Why are you here?" she murmured. "I mean at the hotel."

"You," he answered, sitting on the edge of the bed closest to them, then sipping his Coke.

"Me?"

He looked at her directly. She had noticed him doing that since they'd met, just looking at her directly, unflinchingly, as though it was no problem. It made her uneasy. She was used to other sorts of people who didn't look so closely, who were perhaps more comfortable only seeing what they thought should be there. "I felt you, sensed you, driving near where I worked. So, I followed you. It felt as though something was terribly wrong."

She looked down at her Sprite, breathing deeply. It was easy to talk to him, and for her that was more than unusual. "Where do you work?" That wasn't the question she wanted to ask. But it was the one she could manage.

"Branson, I'm a psychologist."

She glanced up. He had brown eyes, not hard, but still focused on her. "Then you must think I'm crazy."

"No," he said with a bit of surprise. "But I think you're having a difficult time. You should sleep here tonight, in the other bed."

She'd expected it, but still — "Peter, I don't know how I can do that."

"I don't know how you can't," he stated flatly.

Do you need help?

"I don't know."

Have things stabilized?

"I'm not sure about that either."

She slept restlessly, tossing, murmuring in her sleep. He concentrated on her, trying to place a protective shield or rather a bubble of energy around her, but he wasn't sure if he was trying to keep something out or trying to keep her within. And on top of everything, just attempting to maintain it was incredibly draining to him. It was a battle. Clearly, there was an unconscious component of her that wanted to travel, wanted to slip into these other lower, problematic dimensions so close to their own. Yet, her conscious self resisted and was being dragged unwillingly along.

What was happening was terribly disturbing, but beyond that, the why of it bothered him even more. There was a persistence, perhaps a self-destructive thread here, that he did not understand. Peter sat cross-legged on his bed, focusing on her, dropping to a level where he could reach her subconscious mind.

"Nina," he summoned. He felt a stillness overtake her, and the restless thrashing of her sleep ceased. Again, he directed the thought to her mind. *"Nina, do you hear me?"*

The whisper came floating tentatively back to him. *"Yes."*

"What are you fighting?"

There was silence, then a stirring. *"I am drawn."*

"Drawn to what?" he prodded.

"There is something here, something dark."

"Why are you drawn to it?" he asked, pushing her for concreteness.

"I need to stop it."

He hesitated. He hadn't expected this, that there might actually be a purpose to any of her traveling. *"You're very weak."*

"You're stopping me."

"Yes, I don't want anything to happen to you." This was the concern, and he'd openly admitted it, perhaps for the first time to himself. There was something about her, about Nina Ascher, that he was finding it difficult to keep professionally detached from.

"I have to go. Let me."

He stopped, considering. Whether he wanted it or not, it was clear that she would be traveling. *"Let me go with you."*

It seemed like endless moments before there was an answer. Then finally, *"Yes."*

He sent out a call for aid to help bolster him before he released the shield around her. It was clear. If this was really going to happen, then he needed all the help he could get.

Was it shame? She wondered why it was never spoken of. The women of her family seemed to bury their ability as if it were an aberration. They operated under a definitive pressure to blend in, be unseen, appear normal.

But she wasn't. And at times, in wandering the darkness and in exploring these unknown spaces between, she admittedly felt more herself than when she was in the "normal" world.

She landed on a swampy surface, her feet sinking and then rebounding. It was different here, in Peter's hotel room, than it had been in hers. The shadowy, turbulent surfaces were slashed with waves of calming blue-green light, flickering and tempering the darkness.

She recognized from some inner compass that it was temporary. Peter had brought the serene light with him — his influence, his power perhaps. Straightening up from a crouching position, she canvassed the room. As her vision cleared, surprisingly, she saw him right beside her, though he appeared insubstantial, as though he hadn't fully made the leap.

"Are you all right?" She sent the thought toward him. She could almost see its physical movement appearing as a kind of wave in the thick, gelatinous atmosphere.

His image beside her seemed to solidify a bit as her thought merged into him. He began to move, and she saw fluctuations in the light bands. It was clear that all that energy was connected to him.

"Adjusting," he sent to her. And again, she could see the thought traveling in a ripple through the jelly-like atmosphere until it hit her. Although it wasn't exactly a hit, it felt more like a benevolent warmth spreading over her before the meaning crystallized in her mind.

She silenced her thoughts and listened. The buzzing that she remembered from her room was in the distance but near. With instinct, she began to move toward the door, but his arm shot out in front of her, barring her way. "Wait. Where are you going?"

She stopped. She hadn't thought, just responded to the pull. "I need to find it."

Again, his thought collided with her. "Why?"

Why? That repeated in her mind. There wasn't a coherent answer. She didn't know *Why*. She only felt an urgency. She pulled away, forcing her way through the pulsating barrier that was his door. Peter was following her. That much she knew. His thoughts and emotions were tangible things wrapping around her like a cocoon.

Complete disorientation was what Peter was experiencing. The first time that he'd sent himself to this level to reach her, it hadn't been wholly him, just a projected piece of his consciousness. But now, he was all in and woefully out of his element.

He followed her through the sticky mess that was his doorway and into the hall. His vision here was severely compromised. He had experienced moments of complete blindness, then, after periods of settling, some splotchy forms had begun to creep in.

The usual guidance he received from others on his team had become completely muffled out. This place that Nina Ascher had slipped into was clearly a corrosive, toxic space. Just being here had already caused him a severe drain of energy. He had no idea how she continued to function on this level of reality, except that perhaps by virtue of who she was, she possessed a natural immunity to it. Trying to keep up, he followed her down the dark aberration that was the hallway, amazed at how quickly and fluidly she moved in this space, nearly as though she was swimming through the dense atmosphere.

"Where are you going?" he sent out to her.

But she didn't respond, just continued to move, wrapping around unexpected corners and turns. And then suddenly, abruptly, she stopped in front of a doorway. This gave him the chance to finally catch up, reaching her side. She remained motionless, staring forward. From his sketchily representational vision, she now seemed to be floating, feet not even touching what could loosely be called the hallway carpet.

"What is it?" he sent out. Though at first, she didn't seem to respond to him.

"My room," she sent back jarringly. So odd how he could feel the actual impact of her words. "It's inside."

He looked at the fluctuating doorway, now semi-recognizing it in its mutated form. "What does it want?" He sent toward her.

Then she turned to him, no expression. So strange how different she seemed here, more confident, oddly in her element. "It wants me."

Peter wasn't doing well. She could feel it. She knew she should attempt to send him back, but for some reason, his presence was helping her, helping her feel more focused than she usually did, more empowered in some way.

As he stood next to her, she felt an inexplicable impulse that she seemed helpless to resist. Reaching her hand out, she grasped his tightly. Initially, the effect was as expected, skin touching skin, as it would be in their "normal" world, but then, just like the doorways and everything else here, she felt the surface give way. Her flesh began to actually part and melt into his, and she moved beneath the surface of his palm. Her hand began to physically merge with him, sinking past skin, past bone, beyond.

She could feel, feel all that energy she had seen in the room, touching her. And then she sunk deeper, her form, the body that she remembered, completely merging into his, until vision was not hers, nor his, but theirs.

"What is this? What are we becoming?"

"We're one." Each thought was not hers, nor his, but now undeniably theirs.

They moved, though in what form was now unknown. They moved through the doorway, then beyond.

It was there, as expected, waiting in the middle of the room for them. It had drained all the energy she had left behind and grown to enormous proportion, now almost reaching the ceiling in stature.

They knew that they could not leave it like this. It would be too damaging in this world and theirs. They centered thought, drawing from both consciousnesses.

The creature almost immediately began to react, nervously twittered, clearly intimidated by what they'd become. It felt them, and its great misshapen head twitched in agitation.

With all the force they could muster, they directed energy, his energy, her focus, with the solitary thought of evolution. The thing that had been a fly in her room was hit, at the center of its being, scrambling, maddeningly for a moment in response to the flood of positive energy, then stopping and finally allowing the evolution to take place. It shrunk and transformed before them, mutating into a small form, a bird, perhaps a sparrow, that fluttered uncontrollably for a moment, then flew out of the room from a sudden gap that appeared in the wall.

They stood there, transfixed by what they'd done. Then Nina began to feel the tearing of their separation before everything swirled into blackness.

She was unconscious when he found her on the hotel room floor, breathing steadily though her pulse was racing. Peter shakily placed her in one of the beds pulling the blanket over her. He was trembling from the profound loss of energy. What had occurred, he couldn't even begin to wrap his mind around. Profound didn't even begin to scratch the surface. He'd always been drawn, drawn to the paranormal, drawn to the otherworldly elements of his studies. And undeniably, he'd been drawn to Nina Ascher even before he set eyes on her. But now, well, they were connected in a way that he couldn't begin to fathom. At the moment, though, all he wanted to do was rest. He hesitated, then climbed into the bed himself, pulling her into his arms before he collapsed into sleep.

What happened?

"It's hard to say. We were able to intercept a drainer on another dimensional level and, well, stop it."

Stop it. How?

He paused. How could he explain? How could he explain something that he didn't understand?

Nina had woken up during the night a few times. She seemed a bit disoriented, but other than that, in reasonable health. He had made a motion to leave the bed, but she'd held onto his arm, pulling him back. There weren't words. What had happened between them was beyond words. They had become one being, one being that had the power to evolve another creature out of its own darkness into a new form of existence. He couldn't imagine what that meant going forward — only that a formidable link had been forged between them.

She'd slept the rest of the night in his arms. Tomorrow they'd talk, talk about how to move forward, how they would move forward together.

"It's hard to explain. I think we'll need a bit of time to sort things out, sort out the ramifications. But I'll be in touch."

The Storm

The rain was pouring down in sheets, bands, they were called. She watched pensively through her balcony door. The breeze felt good, flooding into the dimly lit room. She stared downward toward the inner courtyard of the Hotel St. Helene from the second floor. The swimming pool below, situated just in the center of the ornate patio, rippled with the cascading rain droplets. The news said that the tropical storm should move over quickly, just tying up things for a bit, though the establishment had taken the precaution of placing sandbags at all its entrances.

It was unexpected.

The storm was in the Gulf of Mexico but was predicted to move into Texas. Surprisingly, at the last minute, it took a jog to the right and landed in Louisiana, crashing her weekend getaway. She knew there might be a bit of rain, and it was the middle of hurricane season, late September, but she had been reluctant to shift course. She needed this. This time signaled a personal emancipation of sorts, beginning her life anew, and now, consequently, she was trapped in this little boutique hotel in the French Quarter for who knew how long.

She thought about going downstairs, not just staying here, trapped in the room. Though admittedly, it was a lovely trap, atmospheric. It reminded her of another time, one well removed from everything that her life represented to her now.

That voice in the back of her head, the cautious one that usually governed, suggested that perhaps she should shut the balcony door, but the breeze felt so lovely, and lifted her spirits. There was a rebelliousness burgeoning up inside, one she usually kept in check, that seemed deliberately at odds with all those things she should do.

Undeniably though, the best part of this excursion was that no one knew where she was. For the next two days, she'd escaped the snare of familial interference, people telling her what she should do, how to get on with her life, how she should feel. One way or another, this would be the new beginning for her that she so desperately craved.

It was a time to shed her old life, although, at the moment, all that progressive intent forward was a bit stymied as she was stuck in the middle of a storm. In some respects, storms made everything stand still. The world and all her desires would simply have to pause until it passed over.

Then again, perhaps this was just what she needed, a moment of quiet, suspended expectation.

She leaned back on the white bedspread and closed her eyes, fatigue overtaking her. It had been this way for some time, just fatigue. She was so tired of stress, tired of her life as it was. Undoubtedly, it was purely emotional or perhaps not.

He prowled with a deliberate restlessness. That was really the only way he could describe it. He felt the clerk's eyes on his back as he watched the torrents of rain pouring onto the street outside the plate glass windows. "Shouldn't this be boarded up?" he fired toward the desk clerk, perhaps a little abrasively.

"It's only a tropical storm, sir. It should pass over with no incident."

He frowned with tangible irritation. He was on a business trip traveling from up North. This whole thing was woefully unexpected. "*Only*" a tropical storm was significant enough to cancel all his meetings and trap him in this little hotel. With frustration, he stalked the length of the antiquated lobby again.

"Would you like more coffee, sir?"

He looked down at the Styrofoam cup in his hand that had been already filled twice with coffee several times stronger than he would ever obtain back home. The young clerk, a slender lad that couldn't have been more than in his early twenties, had made a pot of coffee just half an hour ago when he'd showed up. This storm was bothering him, and he undoubtedly was bothering the young desk clerk. "No, that's all right." Clearly, he was jumpy enough.

Mathias West didn't like feeling trapped. He couldn't book a flight out early, and he couldn't roam the streets of New Orleans because of the storm. And he didn't want to stop moving because if he did, it would only remind him of things he didn't feel like facing, for instance what a hollow sort of shamble his life was at present. Ostensibly, he was a workaholic. He dated casually with no real intent at permanency, frankly, because it was easier and had become a habit. And usually, he was so busy that none of that was a problem unless, of course, things stopped — like now.

He definitely did not want this quiet time to reflect, but it seemed mother nature had other things in mind. So instead, he continued to stare out the window at the sheets of rain cascading off the pavement of Chartres St., trying to will it to move on, knowing full well what a futile waste of energy that was.

"Is there coffee?" He heard a decidedly feminine voice in the vicinity of the front desk. Turning around, he spied a tall slim, brunette woman at the small coffee station on the side of the long cherry wood desk. Amazing, another soul stirring in this bleak situation.

"How is the storm?" He heard her ask the young clerk, but he interrupted, answering rather intrusively.

"Wet and unmoving."

Slowly, she turned around at the sound of his voice. Yes, tall, slender, pale skin, and enormous eyes, lovely, he registered rather quickly. "Oh really, not moving?" she asked with surprise.

"Umm, no, Ma'am, actually," the young clerk intervened. "The storm is moving. It will just take a day or so to completely clear out."

He shrugged, turning back to the window, "Best listen to the expert," he muttered.

And then, surprisingly, in just a few moments, she was standing next to him, coffee cup in hand. "I know it's an inconvenience, but I do love the rain," she murmured.

"This much of it?" he asked with sarcasm.

"I suppose that seems odd. But I find it, well, energizing, I suppose." He couldn't help but pick up on it. There was something just a bit wistful in her voice as well as a lovely intonation that seemed only characteristic of New Orleans, or so he'd surmised in the brief time he'd been in the city.

"Well, as it seems, we'll be stranded here for a bit. I suppose I should introduce myself, Mathias West." He didn't bother to outstretch his hand as both were still holding coffee cups.

"What an interesting name," she commented softly. "Olivia Blanchard," she offered, smiling at him only briefly. And there was no denying it. Just that quickly, he was intrigued.

The small restaurant in one corner of the Hotel St. Helene opened around 7:00 AM. And as it was, they were the only partakers of breakfast. "I've been told to caution you that the hotel could lose electricity at any moment." The young blond waitress told them rather gravely.

Liv smiled, sipping her orange juice. Across from her, her breakfast companion just gave a sort of grunt in acknowledgment. "Thank you," Liv murmured just before the younger girl scurried away. Liv herself was only thirty-five, but these days she felt like Methuselah next to some of these young kids. Across from her, Mathias, she was still trying to wrap her brain around that name, drank his coffee. She wondered how he could drink so much of it, but then again, he did strike her as someone living a bit on the edge of things. "You know. It may just blow over with no power outages. It's usually the wind that does damage and, of course, the flooding."

He nodded, "So I've heard. We get our share of storms, so they're not completely alien to me. I just wasn't expecting one here. Now, I mean. There wasn't enough warning. It really threw a kink into things."

"Yep, they do tend to get in the way," she responded with the slightest tinge of humor in her voice. She was surprised to be sitting here with this man, this odd, cantankerous sort of individual. He'd caught her unaware in the lobby, striking up a sort of pessimistic conversation about the weather when she'd joined him in watching the tropical storm roll in through the front window of The Hotel St. Helene. "I'm sure tomorrow things will right themselves again."

"Can I quote you on that, Olivia?" he'd said a little gruffly, though he lingered on her name a bit. He wasn't really what most people would consider a handsome man — probably at least in his forties, bearded, with dark brown hair, more on the husky side than slim, just a little taller than her, under six feet, she thought, and exuding, what was it, a sort of direct, disgruntled demeanor. An angry bear, she'd thought to herself, but it didn't bother her. She was a teacher and used to fielding all types of personalities.

"No, you better not, just in case I end up being wrong."

He'd looked at her then a little oddly, assessing, she thought. Most people tended to dig in on their opinions, but she wasn't nearly that committed to off-handed remarks. "Are you local?" he asked.

"Yes," she smiled, "native to New Orleans."

"I could almost pick up that peculiar accent. It's not exactly Southern."

She smiled, amused at being described as peculiar. "Well, southern covers a lot of territory. Though I admit we're different than mostly anything else around us. And you are from?"

"Up North, Maryland originally, now Boston. I am, well, was in for a convention, supposed to be a sort of vacation."

"Thus, the frustration," she murmured lightly.

And it continued on, small talk. He worked for the Boston Globe, an editor, and she, a teacher at a community college. She expected him to be dismissive of that, many were, but he wasn't. Just continued to ask more questions. Of course, she didn't flatter herself that he was really interested. It was clear to her that Mathias West quite desperately needed a distraction, and she just happened to fit the bill at the moment. After all, in truth, a distraction suited her as well.

She sipped her cool frothy sort of orange juice and thought how lovely and indulgent a Mimosa would be just now. Glancing around the small restaurant, she noted that she and Mathias West were indeed the only individuals here. So strange, she hadn't even intended to leave her room that morning, but then the strongest restlessness had flooded over her, a need to ramble and explore, so much that it felt impossible to resist. So, she didn't. After all, she was now a free agent of the freest kind.

"Well, Olivia Blanchard," he said casually, stirring his coffee, "you haven't told me if there is a Mr. Blanchard."

The question jolted her a bit, but then again, she'd forgotten that the angry bear was direct and had no southern sensibilities of tactfulness, a quality which actually suited her just now. She was tired of careful people. "No, no, Mr. West, just me."

Mathias waited, looking at her for an instant as though expecting her to continue, then finally filled in. "Well, Olivia, I should tell you that I wasn't always an editor. I started as an investigative reporter in my younger days and can't shake the feeling that your response wasn't a hard "No" but rather a soft one."

"A soft one?" she questioned.

"More story there," he elaborated.

She glanced around, wishing distractedly the waitress would come with her hash browns and eggs. She didn't usually eat much breakfast, but for some reason, she felt like indulging, just like the hotel, an indulgence. Oh yes, back to his prying, "I'm not sure what you mean, Mathias." She said softly with an elusive smile but then noticed that he was studying her quietly, probably waiting for an answer that sounded reasonable. Well, she shouldn't be surprised. Again, what else was he going to do today except perhaps dig up a stranger's skeletons in the closet. "I'm recently divorced," she offered quickly.

He nodded slightly as though she'd only acknowledged what he'd picked up on. "Yep, divorce is its special kind of hell, never easy."

"Personal experience?" she asked, not overly concerned if she was now prying. It was only fair, and tactfulness seemed out the window here. It wasn't as if they ran in the same circles or ever would. So, what if she offended him? Though oddly, her impression was that offending him might be difficult to do.

"About eight years ago, we'd been married just out of college, then, well, it just sort of fell apart."

"My husband and I had been married just short of ten years. It was final, I guess, about a month ago."

"Children?" he asked calmly.

"No, I, well, we tried. I lost a baby close to term once. Then there was another miscarriage. Just didn't seem to be in the cards."

His eyes seemed to change a bit. They were light-colored, maybe blue or green. She wasn't sure. "That must have been difficult," he said, maybe in a comforting way. It was difficult to tell with him. It wasn't his nature to comfort, she suspected, but she could be wrong. She didn't have the best track record in reading people, her ex-husband being a prime example.

"Yes, it was, but the marriage wasn't good. Children would have — I don't know."

"Made it complicated?"

She sighed, smiling a bit. Funny feeling confiding in a stranger. It wasn't her nature to be so unguarded. But here, now, with the storm, in this lovely little hotel so far apart from the way she'd always lived, it didn't seem to matter all that much. "I would have loved children, but yes, it would have made it difficult. Ryan and I were leading separate lives. And he, well, just went off and fell in love with someone else."

His eyes were so fixed on her as though he was intently listening to what she was saying. It was odd that amount of attention. "I'm sorry, Olivia. That sounds like a very painful time."

She smiled, "Most people I know call me Liv. Olivia seems very formal."

He nodded, "Liv," as though considering if, indeed, he felt comfortable with the sound of it on his lips, and then the food arrived, and the intense conversation stopped for the moment.

The storm continued to rage outside. Once and a while, he could hear it pattering, but it felt different now. All the irritation, the frustration he was indulging earlier, was being stripped away. Liv? Did he dare tell her he preferred Olivia? Did he dare tell her that she was entrancing him with her candidness, with the lovely intoxicating tone of her voice? That a forty-three-year-old man was developing an intense infatuation with a perfect stranger, with emphasis on the word perfect.

This was ridiculous at his age. But he wanted to excoriate the ex-husband, and he wanted to thank him profusely for letting her go and throwing her in his path. She was quiet now, eating her breakfast, and he knew she was wondering if she'd made a mistake sharing that very raw and painful part of her life that she was still dealing with. He knew people, how to read people. But this, what was going on here, was new. He was a middle-aged man, and he felt as though he was in entirely new territory. "So, you're leaving tomorrow?" she asked, her eyes wide. They were hazel, with flecks of dark green throughout.

"I'm not sure. There was a convention, and meetings scheduled through the weekend, but I have a feeling all of it might be canceled."

She smiled, "Pity you can't see more of the city. Have you been here before?"

"No, I haven't. I wasn't planning much sightseeing, but I could be stranded for a little while."

"There are worse places to be."

He moved his scrambled eggs around on the plate a bit. He'd ordered as she had, not really hungry and right now not at all interested in his food. And then he asked the question he'd been wanting to ask for some time now. "So, you live here in New Orleans, Liv?"

"Yes, well, in Jefferson, I have a townhouse."

"So, you're here at this hotel. Why exactly?"

She paused, looking at him strangely. She was used to being judged. He could feel her wariness on his skin. He did have instincts, as he called them. "I guess that seems strange to you."

"No, not necessarily. I'm just curious, trying to put all the pieces together."

"Pieces?"

"Lovely woman, all alone in this little boutique hotel buried in the French Quarter. I'm just nosy, I guess."

She smiled again tentatively, looking down at her plate, then glancing up at him almost shyly, deciding whether to trust him, perhaps deciding whether it mattered if she could or not. "I just needed something different, a break, away from the old life — from people, from old things. I wanted something for me, completely out of the ordinary. I guess that sounds a bit self-indulgent."

He shook his head slowly. "No, I booked this hotel away from the convention center, away from people I might know for something different as well. To breathe different air for a little while."

She stared at him, considering, he thought, that maybe under all his gruffness, there might be something there, something quizzically kindred. "That's it exactly, to breathe different air. You do understand."

"Yes, of course I do, Olivia."

He left the doors leading out to the balcony open in his room. The breeze from the rain outside helped to keep the room cooler. Just after his entrancing breakfast with Olivia Blanchard, the building did indeed lose electricity. He and Olivia had taken the stairs to the second floor, where they both resided. He'd escorted her to her room at the other end of the hall, wondering distractedly how to prolong their exchange.

"Are you a fan of cards?"

She'd smiled, indulgently he thought. "Only if I'm winning."

"I travel with a deck. Seeing as we're a bit trapped here, maybe I can test your skill later."

She stood in the narrow hallway, looking at him in a way that made him wish they weren't parting just now. "That sounds intriguing, Mr. West. You know where I am." And then she'd left him to his own devices. Oddly, he wasn't thinking anymore about his frustration of being trapped here, unable to get on with things. Now, he was thinking about how long to wait before going down the hall to knock on Olivia Blanchard's door.

The opened balcony doors allowed some light to creep into the hotel room. Outside, the storm raged, but she felt as though that veil of depression hanging on her for months had been lightened. She smiled to herself. Suddenly, she felt young again, engaging, attractive. "Angry Bear," she laughed, thinking about the man just down the hall that seemed anything but that now. In the short time they'd spent together downstairs in the lobby, then the dining room, she'd begun to see beneath the layers. He was incredibly sharp, to the point, insightful, compassionate, funny, and incredibly good-looking, and he was leaving for Massachusetts in probably a day. She was being silly, but it felt so good to be seen for a change, to be listened to, to not be judged by a lifetime of baggage.

She stood by the open doorway, feeling the soft mist of rain caressing her face. She was tired, but she didn't want to sleep. She wanted to jump in headfirst. Of course, she didn't know his room number. Maybe she could figure it out. And then, a bit unexpectedly, she heard a soft knock.

She whisked open the hotel door without hesitation. He was standing in the hallway with a deck of cards in one hand and a can of cashews in the other. "I picked these up at the airport. They're my weakness. But I can come back later if you'd like to rest."

"No, maybe it's the storm, but I'm restless. Come in. We can pass the time," she said tentatively.

And then he looked at her warmly, making her melt a bit inside. This probably wasn't the best idea and wasn't safe, but she craved, needed to feel alive for a change.

As the day stretched on, the rain continued to pound outside the hotel with shifting levels of intensity. But it went unnoticed as they whiled away the morning playing cards first on the coffee table that stretched in front of the white loveseat in what she would term the sitting room of her tiny suite, then later across the great white puffy comforter of her double bed, as it was more comfortable for leaning and resting with the large down stuffed pillows.

Was it improper?

The idea had not even crossed Olivia's mind. She should be more careful. She supposed. After all, what did she really know about this man, except that he was good at poker, not at gin, and a bit clueless about stealing casino, though he did seem to be catching on.

She was sitting on the bed, shoes off, leaning back against the headboard while Mathias sat at the foot, leaning on one arm. He'd gotten rid of his sports jacket early on and rolled up the sleeves of a button-down blue shirt as the room was definitely getting stuffy from the lack of air. They'd both gotten bottles of water from the mini fridge, taking advantage while it was still cool.

Her mother would think her mad, allowing a stranger to spend so much time in her hotel room, but at the moment, she didn't wish to think about her mother. And her less-than-supportive antics during her separation.

"So, I can pick up the ten and the two cards that add up to it," he said with an intent expression that made her want to giggle.

"Yes, all that."

He glanced up with a furrowed brow. "Now, don't laugh at me. I'm an amateur here."

"No, Mathias, I saw you play poker. I definitely wouldn't call you an amateur. So, no one ever calls you a nickname, just Mathias?"

He nodded solemnly, still focused on the cards. Evidently, he was taking this very seriously. "Yes, nothing ever seemed to fit me. So, I was stuck with Mathias."

She sipped the water that was now becoming less than cool. "It's going to get pretty muggy in here with no air."

He straightened up, picking up his pile of cards and adding them to a very meager stack on the side. "Yes, I've noticed that about your climate here, very sultry."

"The word is humid, and yes, it can be daunting even in the Fall."

"The Fall is lovely up north," he murmured. "You should come see it."

She looked at him a bit oddly. The talk had been rather superficial, nothing as deep as what they'd perused over breakfast. But she'd felt a slight shift in his tone. "I've been up as far North as North Carolina, but that's it."

"Your turn," he said. Then as she quickly picked up a card, he added, "I'd be happy to show you around Olivia Blanchard if you'd like to see it."

She glanced up with a bit of surprise. That was direct, but then again, that was him, quite direct. "But you barely know me, Mathias," she said lightly, taken aback by the draw she felt to this "stranger." But a "stranger" who undeniably felt like someone remarkably familiar.

And then, quite unexpectedly, he reached out, covering her hand with his, and she felt an overwhelming response to the sudden contact. Was it attraction? She didn't know. She'd never felt this before, this soothing feeling emanating into her skin through his touch, electric, maybe, but calming, mesmerizing. "Oddly, doesn't feel that way."

She hesitated, nodding a bit, acknowledging the unchartered nature of their situation. Was she being silly? Probably, but she felt inclined to push away all those fearful voices that difficult life experiences had hammered into her head, the ones telling her to second guess everything she felt or thought, the ones telling her that somehow she was unworthy of feeling good or having happiness. All of them felt so easy to drown out in the moment.

"You're thinking way too much, Olivia," he murmured. His voice had that rich, deep timbre that seemed to reach inside her.

She smiled shyly, "Picked that up, did you?"

He squeezed her hand a bit. "I can literally feel it on you and, of course, see it in your eyes. They're so easy to read."

"Guileless," she muttered.

"I would have said entrancing." And then he reached over, lightly touching her face and pulling her in for the softest kiss. She couldn't remember what she should do, couldn't remember who she was before this moment, only that she sank into the comfort, sank deeply into the possibility.

Olivia knew things, knew she should stop, knew this would probably end in heartbreak for her if she let herself — what was the word, feel.

"It's all right," he whispered, pushing the cards onto the floor of the hotel room and pulling her closer to him, his hands on her sides.

She breathed in deeply. What could she do? What did she want to do? Again, his mouth was on hers, more insistent, magnetic, pulling her intently toward him. And then there was the swirl, like the storm outside, that just blotted away everything, blotted away memory, concern, and allowed her to respond as if this moment between them was all there was.

She kissed him back, pulling him more securely to her, against her. All was forgotten, and all was remembered as they began to find peace and healing in each other's arms.

He quietly watched her lying next to him asleep. Mathias could still hear the storm raging outside. The doors on the balcony patio were partially opened. But inside the room, it was calm. He was perfectly content to be still now. He wasn't thinking to the next moment, rushing onward, plotting, strategizing beyond this place. It was perfectly novel to him. He was content.

She shifted in her sleep, then her eyes fluttered open. They were so lovely, deep, warm, compassionate, and vulnerable. He remembered holding her so close just a little while ago, the passion and gentleness in her eyes as he made love to her. He wasn't the sort of man who liked to deceive himself, and it was clear, even to him, that he'd fallen in love, maybe for the first time in his life. What a predicament, what a glorious predicament.

She moved again beside him, then murmured. "What time is it, Mathias?"

"I have no idea," he whispered huskily, reaching over to her again and pulling her against him. He was determined now, determined to pull everything this moment had to offer.

She was hungry. On and off during the evening, they had raided the mini-fridge in her room. Then he had done the same in his returning with an assortment of cookies and crackers. And they had lived off of these for the rest of the evening, between, well, between passionate bouts of making love.

Olivia didn't concern herself with birth control. She'd been told after her last miscarriage that it was unlikely that she would conceive again. And she hadn't really tested that diagnosis until today.

"Any chance we could find something else to eat downstairs?" she asked.

Mathias was across the room looking out the balcony wearing his shirt untucked over his pants. For the balance of the day, they'd worn a lot less. It made her cheeks warm. Even when she'd been married, she couldn't remember having spent such an intensely intimate day. She pulled the sheet up a little higher, noting that she was completely naked beneath. "I suppose we could get dressed and go foraging."

She laughed, "Sounds like a lot of effort. How does it look out there?"

"Still raining, still wet, but the sun is trying to make its way out."

"Too bad, I've decided yesterday was my favorite day ever. Don't really want it to end."

He turned back to her, sitting on the edge of the bed, then taking her hand in his. "My favorite day ever as well, Olivia. But it doesn't have to be the only one."

She smiled. She didn't want to think about it, didn't want to think about what this meant, could mean, anything really. She just wanted to continue to be simply happy. "Why don't you come back to bed, Mathias?"

"I thought you were hungry."

She pulled on his arm. "It will keep." And he complied rather easily, she thought.

Afterwards, they slept again. And Olivia dreamed of the storm. She could see it rolling over the landscape, not like a usual hurricane but like a great steamroller of turbulent clouds breaking through the land, through her townhouse where she lived, through the school where she taught, her car, her mother's house, the quaint little house where she used to live with Ryan uptown. All of it was crushed, demolished, with nothing left. It was devastating, but strangely she didn't feel devastated. She felt relieved as all those old bondages that weighed her down were purged from the landscape, and she was left stripped, naked, ready to start over.

She woke up with a start. Mathias was not next to her, and her heart lurched in panic. Maybe he'd left. Maybe he'd decided their "fun" night was over. Then she heard rattling in the bathroom, and he walked out.

She bunched the bedsheets in her hands but didn't feel relief. "I didn't want to wake you," he said, smiling. Then his expression changed as he sat beside her on the bed, "What's wrong?"

"Honestly?" she asked.

"Of course," he said, lightly brushing her face with his fingertips.

"For a moment, I thought you'd left."

"Really? Why would you think that?"

"I don't know. This, last night, yesterday, it's all new territory for me. Was it a fling? Two people trapped in a storm whiling away the time. Or, or was it—"

"Something more," he filled in. "What do you want it to be, Olivia?"

"I think I want you to tell me what you want it to be first," she stammered. "This is all scary for me. I'm quite sure I don't have to say this, but it's not my normal way of doing things."

He took her hand, murmuring, "No, no, you don't have to say it. I don't want you to feel afraid. Honestly, it's new territory for me as well. I can't ever remember feeling this way, feeling such a profound draw to someone as I do to you."

"So, what now?" she whispered.

"We need to talk and make plans. I want you to come back to Boston with me."

She leaned back against the pillows. "Really, just like that?"

He nodded slowly, "Yes, just like that, I can take some time off, several weeks, spend it helping you to get things in order, then we can go."

"Just upend my life."

His expression hardened a bit as though he was considering. "Is it a life worth preserving?"

She frowned at his bluntness. "I don't know Mathias. That's a lot of change."

"You asked what I want. I think I'm making it clear that I want you."

"So, I move to Boston. What, then, we live together? I'm not really keen on that."

"Then let's get married."

"I just got unmarried."

"Then I'll find you a place there for a while and help you find a job until—" he sighed deeply, running his hand through his thick hair. "Look, I haven't had the time to figure this out beyond I want to be with you, perhaps need to be with you, Olivia. The question is, what do you want."

She pursed her lips. Old habits die hard. She was afraid, afraid to leap. "Right now, I want to get dressed and get something to eat." Suddenly, she heard a quick sizzle, almost like a zap, and then the electricity flashed on.

He looked up a little darkly she thought, "Well, I guess we're back to real life," he commented dryly.

Mathias plugged in his cell phone, whose battery had depleted sometime before and showered. He'd left Olivia in her room to do the same. He'd thought about suggesting they do so together but then sensed that she needed a little time to herself to consider what they'd discussed.

For him, it seemed obvious, quite black and white. They should be together, even if that meant uprooting her to do it. Maybe her roots here were deeper than he suspected. Maybe it was an old habit, being comforted by the familiar, even if it was miserable, though he hoped this was not the case.

But the time they'd spent together had been a revelation for him. He was old enough to be able to sense the extraordinary. It wasn't just the sex, though he had to admit that it was unparalleled. But it was mostly the astonishing connection he felt just being near her, talking to her. He always heard the word kindred but didn't truly understand what it meant until now.

But he did know how to fight, be tenacious, and get what he wanted. And what he wanted was Olivia Blanchard. He just had to figure out how to convince her.

She dressed slowly, deliberately. They were to meet downstairs in half an hour, and she had to say something. "What do you want, Olivia?" he'd asked. Had she answered? What did she want?

She wanted to go back to last night when everything was simple, and they were just together, with no past, no future.

She thought again about her dream. About the great storm rolling through and pummeling her life. Was that what Mathias was — a great storm flattening her old life? But in the dream, she didn't seem to mind. She felt unfettered, free. All she had to do was take the leap. But did she even have that in her anymore? To leap?

He waited for her in the lobby, noting a different clerk at the desk this morning. A rather tall, dark-haired boy, still young. He passed by the coffee. He didn't want it. He felt more than awake already. Outside, the sky seemed bright and rosy. One would scarcely know that a storm had blown through.

He wandered to the desk, the young man seeming enmeshed in his laptop. "Well, I guess the storm has passed."

The boy glanced up, plastering on a friendly smile. "Sir?"

"The storm from yesterday, the tropical storm, Selene, or whatever they called it. It's passed."

Confusion seemed to furrow his young brow. "Storm, sir? I'm sorry, I don't know what—"

"Now come on. It knocked the lights out last night."

"What's the matter, Mathias?" Suddenly, Olivia was right at his elbow. He hadn't even heard her approach.

"This young man seems to be playing a prank on me. Not very funny if you ask me."

"No sir, I'm sorry. I wasn't here yesterday, but I assure you there was no storm. It was a beautiful sunny day."

"Now look—"

She grabbed his arm firmly. "Mathias, come here. Let's get something to eat."

"Olivia."

"It's all right," she murmured, pulling at him firmly. "It's all right."

"I don't understand," he grumbled. "How ridiculous."

It was quite bizarre. Olivia felt dizzy. She remembered the storm yesterday when the lights were out — all the hours spent together in bed and the weather raging outside. But then she remembered dreaming about the storm, and now suddenly, it all felt confusing.

"You remember it, don't you? When we met downstairs in the lobby, we watched the rain."

Vaguely now, she remembered, but thinking about it made her head spin. Maybe it was hunger. That was why they hadn't eaten, wasn't it? "I—I think so."

Mathias reached into his pocket for his phone. He could check the news. That would confirm it and settle all this nonsense. But then he remembered that he'd plugged it in upstairs. "I have to get my phone."

"I'll wait for you."

"No, no," he said, grabbing her arm. It was ludicrous, but in all the confusion, he didn't want her slipping away as well.

Mathias was a man that hung onto the facts. It made him feel grounded in his work and his life. But now, out of the blue, things felt indefinite, not grounded, as unstable as sand.

He held onto Olivia, pulled her to his side, and wrapped his arm around her in the elevator. She wasn't saying much.

"You do remember, don't you?"

And she whispered, "Yes, of course," but it sounded hesitant. Was he losing it? Had he had some sort of bizarre stroke that tampered with his well-ordered memory?

By the time they got to his room, his head was spinning with disorientation. He moved quickly across the space to the phone on the end table. There were several voicemails. He looked at Olivia with concern, who had immediately sat down on the edge of the bed.

Quickly, he listened intently to the mails. "Mathias, where are you, buddy? You missed the first two meetings at the Conference Center. Are you all right?"

Then, "Mathias, it's after lunch. Are you going to be a no-show all day?"

And lastly, "Mathias, it's Todd. Call me back."

He stared at the phone as if it were a viper and let it slip from his fingers onto the bed. He stared wide-eyed at Olivia. "What's happening?"

She shook her head. "I'm so tired. Can we sleep?" Abruptly, he pulled her into his arms, and they laid down.

Olivia stood on a hill overlooking the city below. It vaguely registered that it wasn't a landscape that was literal but rather symbolic.

"What are we looking at?"

Mathias was beside her this time. "The path of the storm," she answered.

"I don't see it," he stated flatly.

She smiled, "Don't you see it's changed everything, remade what was."

"Has it?"

She took his hand. She could see it clearly, but it might take Mathias a while. But she'd be with him to help.

Slowly, she opened her eyes. Her head pounded, oh yes, with hunger. They still hadn't eaten. Mathias was sitting up beside her, looking around. "I guess I better let them know I won't be making the conference."

She took his hand. "Let's go slow. First, get breakfast, then we'll figure out our next step."

He nodded, pulling up her hand to kiss it. "I can't quite remember Olivia. Was there ever a storm?"

"I think there was, but not exactly the way we thought."

The Armstrong

It was an old hotel. That was something that could be felt, all its history, in fact, on her very skin.

She would have preferred something new, a structure that maybe hadn't been around for so many years. Of course, it was quite impressive with its chandeliers, intricate blue and gold effigies on the ceiling, and vast spaces trimmed with mahogany accents.

But she would have preferred something new, not so vast, not so imposing.

Once she got upstairs, the halls were narrower, not as grandiose, skinny spaces filled with rooms facing each other. Just past the elevator down the long hallway, there was a painting slapped on the wall — an old plantation, she thought, not much consideration. Perhaps someone just thought it looked pretty.

She moved quickly, swiping her room key and slamming the heavy hotel door behind her. She threw her shoulder bag down onto the king-sized bed. Checking her watch, it was late, eight-thirty.

She wasn't entirely sure why she was here, why she'd made the effort. This was pointless. All of it, but she couldn't stop. She had no idea how to begin to stop.

The lobby was quite full when he arrived, having been dropped off by a handsome cab. He had taken a train from his home in New Orleans to Alexandria, and it was well into the evening when he arrived. There were all manner of individuals milling about The Armstrong, evidently being a center of social activity as well as a hotel. A valet had offered to carry his trunk and greatcoat, but he declined. As he took the lift to the third floor, he focused. It was necessary now to achieve great concentration.

Fortunately, the narrow hallway to his room was deserted, unlike the downstairs. It could be any place, anywhere, and more than that, any time. He held the key that he'd been given tightly in his hand. And then he closed his eyes, focusing intently just before he put it in the door.

He allowed himself to be pulled, pulled by the life force he sensed. After all, time is an ephemeral construction. What is genuine power is energy, the magnetism of energy. He allowed himself, his senses, to be drawn, then opened the door.

"Lydia," her eyes fluttered open.

Surely, she'd been dreaming. Then the fatigue swept over her, and her eyes drifted closed again. *"Lydia, focus."*

Someone was talking to her, but she was asleep, wasn't she?

"It's an intermediary state of awareness. Not sleep, not awake. That is how I am able to contact you."

"I—I don't understand."

"It is Charles. I've been trying to reach you for some time."

It had begun slowly, insidiously. There were communications that she could attribute to imaginations, indulgences, then later even mental illness.

At times, they, she and he, would talk at length in that intermediary state. *"You're not ill. You're gifted. There is a vast difference."*

"What is it you want?"

"I want us to meet."

"Meet? How? When?"

He, her apparition, contrivance perhaps, seemed somewhat befuddled by her questions though they seemed more than reasonable to her. In this imagining, he could see her, and she could see him often just across the room. The trouble was that he appeared so insubstantial, passing in and out of vision as though he was made of mist, a fluttering photo on a blanket of vacillating mist.

Befuddled, yes, that was accurate. *"How? Well, yes, that just might be a bit easier than the When."*

"The When?"

"Yes, Lydia." He called her Lydia. Her name was Lilly Finch, but Charles insisted on calling her Lydia. Why exactly? He never made it quite clear.

"I don't understand."

"We need to meet in a particular place. A powerful place in terms of magnetism, raw energy. A place where we can achieve a link."

"What does that mean exactly, a link?"

"It has to do with the When of things."

She was sitting in the corner of the shadowed hotel room, waiting quietly, when the door began to open. It was perfectly reasonable that she should be frightened, terrified really, at what was happening. But she wasn't. She had slipped into the mindset, the altered state that he'd taught her. In fact, it was the very one he had drilled on and on about for nearly an entire year. At first, it had been a few evenings a week, then in the last few months, every day, every day achieving a mesmeric trance that he'd taught her.

And so, she sat serenely as the door to her hotel room swung open. He stepped into the room, not a mist, not part of an imagination, not a dream manifestation, but so very real, in the flesh. Silently, he closed the door behind him, turning a lock that she vaguely acknowledged she did not remember. He placed his black oversized suitcase on the ornate rug covering the wooden floor and draped his long coat over a golden crushed velvet wing-backed chair. She breathed in sharply. She really couldn't help it, somewhat disrupting the very calming influence of the mesmerizing trance. Lilly had suddenly become keenly aware that the surroundings around her had shifted.

The man, Charles, stared at her from across the room. Blond hair, dark eyes, and dressed — again, her breath caught painfully in her throat, dressed in a suit —

"From another time," he finished. She straightened up in the chair that she no longer recognized. He had completed her thought. "It's a side effect," he murmured, "from all the intensive alignment we've been working at."

"Alignment?" she murmured.

"Yes, to make this possible. As I said, the When of things was always going to be more problematic. But we've overcome that, it seems."

She was coming to herself completely now, out of the trance. The room around her had grown. In fact, they were in a sort of sitting room, and beyond an archway, there appeared to be another room. It was a suite, whereas when she'd checked in, she'd been in a single room.

Even the décor had become more elegant — the hotel mahogany furniture, velveteen, and tapestry chairs, paintings of soft country-side scenes, placed on the walls as though someone had given it thought and consideration, she mused distractedly, not just haphazardly hung.

"I don't understand—"

"The place we find ourselves in is a mix of your time in 2019 and mine in 1904," he stated flatly. He was like that, she recalled, from their other unorthodox encounters, very direct.

He had moved closer, standing just in front of her. "It doesn't seem like a mix. It seems to be wholly in your court," she whispered, truly feeling more than a bit overcome.

"There are subtle differences," he said softly, his eyes purely transfixed on her. "Can I take your hand, Lydia?"

"Lilly, my name is Lilly."

"I'm sorry," he held out his hand for her as though she'd already agreed. But she did allow it, allowed him to take her hand, and he rather strongly pulled her to her feet and then into a warm, intense embrace. "I don't know if I believed it was possible to really reach you," he whispered huskily.

It was the writings that he began to find first, in unexpected places, tucked away in books, on his desk, and at times even on the pages of his journal.

The penmanship was distinct, not flowing, and well composed as most writing he'd encountered. But rather rough, and not in script at all, but instead some sort of blockish-looking print.

It's upsetting. I've been having these headaches more often lately. The doctor can't find anything particularly wrong with me, just stress, she said.

He'd found the writing on an unfamiliar stationery stuffed in a book on Animal Magnetism that he was reading by Franz Mesmer.

She even did a cat scan, but nothing. Stress — the convenient diagnosis when they have no idea what is wrong with you. It's frustrating, and I didn't even bother to tell her about the dreams. I suppose that doesn't matter. After all, they are just dreams.

The paper was thin, filled with lines, and the ink was an odd color, a forest green shade. He had no idea where it had come from, perhaps the shop where he'd purchased the book. But such peculiar, abstract content and penmanship.

And then, he found another.

I'm starting a dream journal. Not sure why, except I'm desperate to get things sorted out somehow.

He found this one on the same kind of paper stuffed in the bureau by his bed. He had no idea how it came to be unless the housekeeper or a maid had placed it there. He decided to question them thoroughly the next day as the hour was quite late when he'd discovered it.

Then there was another the following day, in the same piece of furniture, although he was positive it hadn't been there the night before.

Last night, I dreamed I was walking through an unfamiliar house, a large place, very old-fashioned, with a great staircase just past the entrance. I put my hand on the rail, a heavy dark wood, as I ascended to the second floor. As I turned the corner past the stairs, there was a long hallway filled with doors. Then someone was beside me, but I couldn't turn to look. It was like paralysis, but he whispered in my ear in a deep voice. "Which door will you choose, Lydia, or will you return to whence you came?"

It shook him, the name Lydia, such an odd sensation, not a name that was precisely in his memory but rather in his consciousness. It lay, he believed, in a place that existed as a deeper sort of holistic phenomenon attributed to the spiritual plane.

He sunk onto his mahogany four-poster bed. The scrap of paper he held in his grasp was fluttering. And given his usually methodical nature, it was a bit shocking, but his hand was shaking. In fact, not just his hand was trembling. He was trembling all over. He schooled himself to breathe deeply, calmly, but it was next to impossible. His eyes again scanned over the curious script. It felt disturbingly familiar, something he should know or perhaps would know.

Of course, he would check with his housekeeper, Mrs. Farrow, and the two maids, Cecily and Lucy. Of course, he didn't really need to. He was a bachelor, but Lucy was Mrs. Farrow's daughter, and she had asked for her employment as a favor to help her find her way. There was still a slight possibility that it was one of them. He folded the paper over, putting it on the nightstand. It bothered him intensely the name Lydia, but precisely why, well, that continued to elude him.

Her head spun with dizziness. "Try to anchor yourself," he whispered in her ear. She did. She focused on grounding herself within the reality that she was experiencing now. She must first accept that this new place was now her plane of existence.

He continued to hold her, gently rubbing her back soothingly. She didn't know if it was helping or distracting, but she liked it, allowing herself to relax in his embrace. "I cannot tell you how pleased I am to meet you finally," he murmured. And she felt it through his touch. The emotions she felt from him were seeping in through the embrace. "You're so sensitive."

"I—" she started, really having no idea where to begin.

"You must tell your mind that this is real."

She felt her knees buckle as an awareness of her exhaustion swept over her. He swept his hands under her and scooped her up just before she collapsed. "I can't—" she whispered as she lost consciousness.

Exactly when it had all started was difficult to pinpoint, probably the journal. It was supposed to be a dream journal but evolved into something else. She would simply scribble thoughts and feelings in it at odd times during the day. She'd elected to take a semester off from work. She taught English Literature at Loyola University in New Orleans. Her largely inexplicable medical issues had made things too difficult to continue. Kindly, they'd given her time to sort things out, though she was several months in and felt no closer to much of anything being sorted.

One day though, on a chilly day late in September, she'd opened her journal to find the curious writing just below her entry.

What she astonishingly observed was a fine penmanship and a strange sort of ink, completely at odds with her scribble and thick green ballpoint pen.

To Whoever May Receive this. Please take note this is an experiment on my part, an indulgence, if you will. The headaches you are enduring may be connected to a preternatural experience. Do not assume that they are traditionally physiological in the sense that most may encounter.

She remembered staring at the page in total confusion. She, Lilly Finch, lived alone in a townhouse in New Orleans. No one else had access to this journal. Of course, the panic had surged up inside her. Maybe she was losing her mind. Maybe this was some sort of multiple personality disorder. The possibilities that she concocted were quite horrifying. So, she did the only thing she could think of, she answered.

Please tell me. Who is this? You are frightening me.

Two days later, there was an answer in the same formal antiquated script.

Forgive me. My name is Charles Del Couer. I'm a doctor.

Then her response, *How are you doing this?*

And sometime later, an answer. I *found your writings in my bureau several days ago. I believe I am supposed to help you.*

It's difficult to know what to believe and what not to believe once events step out of your ordinary parameter of thinking. Lilly left the journal alone for about a week. She considered all sorts of things, primarily that she was having some sort of a break from reality — schizophrenia, multiple personalities, a brain tumor. But no, they'd done a cat scan. At least the brain tumor wasn't a possibility.

She thought to throw the journal out into the trash. But she couldn't bring herself to. The headaches continued, and she was becoming desperate, desperate for any relief.

Look, I can't deal with much right now. I'm in too much pain. If this is some kind of a trick or worse, if it's just me having some sort of breakdown, then have a little mercy and —

She stopped writing. What else could she say?

She closed the journal and put it on her white desk in the corner of her bedroom, pushing it away for a few moments.

Then tentatively, she slid the old-fashioned looking, leather-bound book she'd purchased from Barnes and Noble back towards her. Taking a breath, she flipped it open to the ribbon-marked page she'd just written on. Just under her writing was a new entry, scribed in that exquisite penmanship. So quickly, it had appeared so quickly now, a response.

Extraordinary.

It began.

So, I believe it falls upon me to convince you that I am not a delusion elicited from the depths of psychosomatic or psychological illness. Very well, so be it. As I explained, my name is Charles Del Couer. I am a practicing physician at the Hotel Dieu, French Hospital, Charity Hospital, and Mercy Hospitals. I am a member of The Society of Magnetism in New Orleans. I live in a house along Esplanade Avenue near the Bayou St. John in Orleans parish.

Some of those hospitals he listed she did not recognize, wasn't even aware had ever existed, but others she did. And the Society of Magnetism, what exactly was that? So how could she create something that she had no knowledge of?

Her head had begun again to pound unmercifully. So, she wrote with a shaky hand.

I'm not trying to insult you. I just must be sure. It's been difficult. She closed her eyes and let the pen drift from her hand, trying to mentally will the pain to subside.

"Breathe deeply."

She could hear the sound, not in her ears, but rather a voice whispering softly in her mind. She followed the advice, regardless of where it was coming from, long measured breaths, in and out.

"Try to focus on allowing the pain to withdraw, to slowly drift away with every breath."

Again, she concentrated, following the directions. With every breath in, she focused, and every breath out, she relaxed, allowing the pain to slowly drain away from her temples and forehead. And it was helping. She could feel it. The pain was still dull but a ghost of the intensity that it had been.

"Good, now, try to lay on your bed and rest briefly. I will continue to focus energy to you."

She didn't reply. She simply groggily did as she was directed to do. She didn't mentally put it together at that moment who was speaking to her, who was directing her. She was just grateful for the help. She drifted effortlessly into sleep, moving into quiet, until she dreamed, dreamed of a great house near the water and the man speaking softly to her.

Dreams became a link between them. It began perhaps that first time when she'd read what he'd written in her journal. And then he'd directed her, helped her, and she suspected mesmerized her into a deep sleep as was his way.

In the dream, she was still in her room, in the bed, but now it was overlaid with a different space — one she didn't recognize. She sat in the bed and saw the enormous mahogany rolltop desk against the wall and the man sitting in a straight-back wooden chair beside it.

He was there but insubstantial, as was his room, quite different from the usual place she inhabited.

"What is this?"

"You should be resting, Lydia, not forcing a connection at this juncture," he answered.

"What does that mean? Forcing a connection?"

His clothes, suit rather was antiquated, and his tie hung loosely undone at the collar of his white shirt. "We, you and I, clearly will be communicating. Somehow we've bridged the space that traditionally separates us."

"Space?" she inquired.

"Yes, space is the only adequate description of what is between us. Time is an artificial construct." Her eyes were examining him. He wasn't old, older than her, but not by much. His hair was a dark blond, and he had a well-kept beard and mustache."

"You're Charles," she murmured.

He studied her intently, with curiosity, she felt because she was feeling so many things. "Yes, yes, I am. You should rest."

"My name isn't Lydia," she said while she felt the fatigue take her over again.

"I know," was the last thing she heard him say.

She slowly opened her eyes but wasn't sure where she'd be when she did so. She felt the pressure of his hand atop hers. Flesh upon flesh, not that insubstantial contact that she'd come to expect between them.

"Lydia," he murmured, softly brushing her hair away from her forehead.

"Charles," she whispered, "where are we? Still in between?"

He whispered under his breath. "Seems so," squeezing her hand, "How are you feeling?"

She glanced slowly around the room, again seeing the ornate vintage furnishings but noting now the tapestry-type wallpaper that she did not remember before. "It's changing," she murmured.

Again, he squeezed her hand. His eyes were blue with amber flecks. She'd never been close enough to him to see that before. They were actually together. It had worked. She hadn't considered if it was possible. She had just worked diligently with him toward that end.

"Yes, it has," he said softly, looking at her with quite a degree of tenderness. He'd read her mind and heard her thoughts as he'd done before. And she remembered now how, along the way, she'd completely fallen in love with him.

"I don't understand how this is possible."

He'd led her through a guided meditation, initially writing his instructions in her journal, then after a few times guiding her with his voice in her mind. Once she had finally achieved that meditative state, he had communicated with thought transference.

"Is this like hypnosis?"

"Not exactly. It travels well beyond simple mesmerism. We have genuinely connected on an astral plane."

And it was dazzling, talking to him as though he was right next to her and sometimes seeing impressions of him in his home, but never truly concrete, always more translucent.

Along the way, she stopped questioning her sanity and simply embraced the process, wherever it might lead.

She was sleeping soundly, and he knew he dare not disturb her no matter how tempted he was. He paced the room, noting that it did indeed seem to be slipping away from her timeline and more into his. He wasn't sure why exactly, only that the environment seemed unstable.

"The headaches, my love, are they worse after our sessions together?"

He didn't know when it had started when he'd started referring to her as my love. It just seemed to have begun organically, and she didn't stop him. It was easy, easy to slip into. She seemed so vulnerable and accessible to him, though wholly insubstantial, like some sort of a dream.

"No, they're actually better after I spend time with you. They crop up when I do other things in the outside world here." He was extremely focused on her as she spoke, having glimpses into her life, flashes of her moving through her environment. And then he went deeper, slipping deeper into the physiology of what was happening.

He could see her in his mind, explicitly see her body in two spaces. In her original plateau, her aura was becoming chaotic, bleeding copious amounts of energy to stabilize itself. There was tremendous stress on her energy systems taking place.

It was disturbing. He questioned if he'd caused this if their contact resulted in this divided stress. But then he remembered that her headaches, as she called them, had begun even before their contact commenced.

"Can't you rest, my love?" he'd asked.

"It's difficult. I'm always tired, bothered, even when I sleep."

"Sleeping isn't always resting, you know," he explained. "Some believe it's traveling to other realities."

"Realities?"

"Yes, this life, this awareness we experience in waking hours, is only a small part of actual living."

"I don't understand."

"Give it time, Lydia," so odd how that name kept slipping out. "Then you will understand."

Of course, she fell in love with him. Why else would she agree to attempt such a thing, such an unthinkable meeting, attempting what rationality told her was impossible? But what was rational and what was not?

She opened her eyes to look around the room. On the bedside table was a platter of fruit and cheese of all types and a bottle of wine next to it.

She sat up shakily in the unfamiliar bed as it wasn't the one that had been there when she initially checked into the hotel. "Are we celebrating?" she murmured.

He was across the room, back to her, staring out a window whose heavy brocade drapes he'd pushed back with his hand. He turned around quickly in response to her inquiry. "How are you feeling?"

She smiled, "I've no clue yet. Dizzy, I guess."

"I thought you'd want to eat something."

He sat beside her on the bed, gently taking her pulse without asking, then lightly feeling her forehead. "Will I live?" she asked with humor.

He squeezed her hand, and she felt that draw to him. She'd always felt it before, but not concrete, not like his flesh next to hers. "You had better. I've put a lot of effort into this."

She smiled softly. "What now, though?" She wasn't sure that she really wanted an answer. If they truly succeeded, that was something they had never really discussed. And now that they had indeed succeeded in bridging the time gap between their worlds, what was on the other side of this moment?

"Why don't you eat something? Then we can talk about things."

She reached over for a strawberry, holding it in her hand momentarily as a peculiar thought crossed her mind. She felt a bit like Persephone, eating the pomegranate seeds in the Underworld. Once she took a bite, would she be unable to go back? Or would she be forever linked to where he was? She looked at him with curiosity, wondering, feeling as though he knew the answer. Though she didn't really hesitate, she didn't and wouldn't regret anything. She simply took a bite.

Variables

There are a thousand different possibilities, a thousand roads one's life can take, hanging only on a moment, a choice, a breath. And, somewhere out there, they're all existing at once.

She turned the corner that led into the lobby of the Great Ozark Inn. And her breath stopped, or so it felt, trapped somewhere inside her heart area. Who had said that love at first sight didn't exist? Surely no one who had truly been in love.

He was standing across the substantial expanse of the rustic lobby in front of the check-in desk, wearing a khaki sportscoat with blue jeans. And he was blond, beautifully blond, and tall, slender with a beard.

Her feet felt quite frozen into the ground, and her head felt as though it spun a bit in disorientation. Grace, Gracie, she whispered to herself. This isn't the time to get cold feet, so she stepped forward but stopped because a woman just standing beside him slipped her hands around his waist, leaning in and whispering in his ear.

It was jarring, a gut punch, particularly how she pressed herself right up against his back, which made her stomach flip. Not because she was jealous, because yes, knowing what she did, yes, she was. But because she could see it. She could see the blue-green life force that was his spiritual energy being pulled right out of him by the Barbie doll drainer.

It gave her chills and tangibly stabbed at her heart area. The woman pulled away from him slightly, then shockingly turned in her direction, staring across the lobby right to where she was tucked away in her corner.

She stiffened her spine and stepped back just a step. This couldn't be right. He was supposed to be alone. Then it came to her abruptly what had happened. She'd been too distracted, too emotional, and wound up in the wrong place. She breathed in sharply and closed her eyes, clearing her mind.

Focus now, Gracie, she coached herself. Find the right one.

It would be easy to say that time rippled, but it wasn't exactly time. Rather it was dimensions. Dimensions shifted almost imperceptibly, a fraction of a space because all possibilities existed so near one another, so remarkably close together.

She couldn't choose with her mind but instead was guided by something else — a sort of internal clock pulling her with instinct to just the right frame.

And then she felt that familiar jolt yanking her to a different reality. She opened her eyes. And then she saw him standing in front of the check-in desk, navy blue jacket this time with khaki pants and no beard. She scoped the area — no tall, shapely blond, just him, alone. She didn't feel anyone with him anywhere near. Because she would, because of who he was to her, she would most decidedly feel the connection.

So, once again, she took a deep breath and then plunged forward.

It was a messy breakup. In fact, a long time coming, but for some reason, he'd let it drag on. Why exactly was hard to articulate. Clearly, he hadn't been thinking straight for some time, but finally, he'd ended it earlier in the month. He used the old excuse: "This isn't working for me anymore. I feel as though I'm moving in a different direction." He didn't say "we." Didn't want to speak for her. Someone had told him that was a bad idea. "Just speak for yourself." Who was that again? Oh yeah, his Mom, many moons before, then it had been a high school breakup. How complicated that had seemed. But how he yearned for those "complicated" days now.

Jess was, to say the least, not pleased with him. They'd been together two years, and she'd seen marriage in their future after a prolonged stint of living together, which, curiously, he'd never allowed to happen. Something deep inside him had just balked at the idea.

Fortunately for him, they didn't work together. He was a freelance graphic artist, and she was a sales rep for a chain of sportswear boutiques. That was how they'd met. So, the break could be clean if she had allowed it to be so.

His head throbbed unmercifully — the headaches, stress, tension, thus the much-needed holiday. It was October in the Ozarks, and the temperature had just dropped a notch. He'd brought his work with him. Maybe he could be more productive away from home, maybe. He'd intended to go further up into the mountains, but something had made him stop here, just an inexplicable pull. He was a great believer in following his instincts, so he'd heeded the impulse.

"Here you go, Mr. Strickland. You're on the third floor."

He glanced up. That was his problem lately, being stuck in his own head. He took the room key cards from the young blond desk clerk. She smiled back at him with a tell-tale interest in her youthful eyes. Early twenties, he'd surmised, probably a good fifteen years younger than him, and besides, he'd sworn off blonds. "Thanks," he murmured, maybe a little aloof, but he felt battered.

"Elevators, just past those doors on the right," she chirped, evidently undaunted.

He nodded with a grunt that he felt sufficed as an acknowledgment and scooped up his two leather luggage bags heading across the lobby. He was so caught up in his myriad thoughts that he didn't notice someone walking just behind him and didn't realize until she entered the elevator beside him. At that moment, he looked up and was a bit surprised. It was definitely not a blond, but rather a redhead, auburn, in fact, petite, willowy, dressed in a longish flowy silky blouse over faded blue jeans with dangly silver earrings. He couldn't help it. She instantly captured his artistic sensibilities.

"What floor?" he asked abruptly, without his usual finesse, as just now, he felt a bit shaken for some reason.

She glanced toward him, large almond-shaped eyes of a greenish sort of tint. "Third," she murmured, soft voice but a lower octave.

"Me too," he commented, probably too friendly. But for some reason, he just couldn't help it.

He wasn't in good shape. She could see it clearly. His energy aura was extremely low.

The drainer, whoever she was, had done a number on him. She felt weak and shivering already from all the energy she was instinctively giving him. It served her right to seek him out like this.

But she couldn't help it. All the dreams, the visions, the past life stuff, she couldn't just allow him to go down the tubes without trying to help.

"So, are you from around here?"

She smiled. He was cute. More than cute, sexy. "Um, more up north, just in for a change of scenery."

He nodded. She noted the dark circles under his eyes. Everything was clearly taking its toll. "Me too, definitely in need of a change of scenery."

The elevator jolted abruptly. Then the silver doors swished open to the third floor. He hesitated, so she stepped out into the rather dimly lit hallway, repositioning her floral tapestry luggage bag, which perched precariously on her shoulder. She hadn't packed well. All of this had been wildly impromptu, not considered, not planned a bit.

She hadn't even told Charlie what she was up to. No doubt she would be put out with her. She walked forward, feeling him moving just behind her. She had to focus. She was here to help, not be drawn into some strange, unpredictable entanglement.

"So, how long will you be here?"

He was suddenly beside her. How he'd managed that in this long skinny hallway, she wasn't at all sure. "Um," she glanced over at the numbers on the doors. Her room was still at least ten away. "Probably just the weekend. I'm a writer and trying to polish some articles. I mean, clean them up."

"Journalist?"

"Yeah, well, sort of, freelance self-help stuff."

"Sounds interesting, I'm a graphic artist." They'd been slowly meandering down the hallway, and she wondered if he was even looking for his room. "By the way, I'm Ely, Ely Strickland."

"Oh, Grace Devlin," she murmured, finally spying her door and wondering if she should just walk by it and continue to talk. But she didn't. She needed to collect herself, so she stopped. "Well, this is me."

"Oh," he looked down at the key card in his hand. "I'm 365, nearly neighbors."

"Nearly," she smiled. They suddenly fell awkwardly silent. What now, Gracie? "So, nice to meet you, Ely."

He just stood there, staring at her blankly. And the moment seemed to stretch on indefinitely. He felt it too. She knew it. That pull, was this stupid putting herself in his orbit? Or was it exactly what she was supposed to do?

"You're where?"

She laid back on the bed. Charlotte, her older sister, had nearly exploded at her just moments before through her cell phone. "Right near the border of Missouri and Arkansas, actually a really nice hotel."

"Good lord Gracie, with some guy?"

"No, I mean, I'm not actually with some guy. We're both here at the hotel. He has his own room, Charlie."

"Elias? Really! And you're sure it's the one you've been tracking."

"I haven't been tracking him, not really. You make me sound like a stalker Charlie. But he's in trouble. He's nearly drained to nothing."

It all sounded so insidious, but the truth was that encountering a bonified drainer was not all that unusual. They were everywhere, could be anyone. It was where the vampire legends came from, but instead of blood, energy was taken. In truth, it was a rung on the reincarnation evolutionary ladder. Everyone spent lifetimes as drainers and also as people who could be drained. There were lessons, things to be learned from both life circumstances.

There was quiet on the other end. "But you're sure, sure it's him?"

"Yeah, I'm sure. I just don't know how I can help. I mean, he's messed up, and I'm nearly tapped out just being near him."

"You're giving him energy, Gracie. That's normal. But if it is him, the question is, how far will you go to help."

She swallowed on a dry throat. She really hadn't thought this through. "On one of the other plateaus/realities, he was still with her. The blond drainer, I mean."

"Yep, and quite possibly could be again if that bond isn't snapped somehow. Of course, if you help him here."

"Then I'll help him in all alternate realities. I know it all bleeds over. But how—"

"I guess you could, well, if you two became involved."

She sat up in the bed, feeling a distinctive flush around her face. "I don't even know him."

"If he is who you say he is, he is the only person in the world you can be close to, safely at least. That link you two have or should have not only protects you but will help you heal him, break the bond with the drainer, and who knows what else."

"So, I just knock on his door and say, by the way, Ely do you want to have a quick fling this weekend with me."

"I didn't really say anything about casual little sister. But you shouldn't worry. If he is who you think he is, then he'll approach you. He won't be able to help himself."

There was a lovely view outside the window of his hotel room. The majestic Ozark mountains rose dramatically on the not-too-distant horizon. He had planned to keep driving until he hit the mountains. But he hadn't. He had stopped here.

And if he hadn't stopped, he wouldn't have met Grace Devlin.

He drew a few lines across the blank page of his twenty by thirty artist pad that he'd brought with him to "get back to basics." But the only thing he was interested in drawing just now was the curve of Grace Devlin's face.

This was stupid. He leaned back against the hard headboard of the hotel bed. He'd just gotten rid of one woman, which was sticky at best. He was more than a bit shocked at the tenacity and, dare he say, anger that Jess had shown during their parting.

He had the daunting feeling that she'd somehow considered him an investment she'd put time and effort into — an investment that had just cut and run.

And the "why" of why exactly he did was a bit opaque even to him. Except when they were together, there was no crackle, no undefinable quality that would feed his inspiration. So, he either had to leave or, sort of settle, settle for a life that he didn't want.

He closed his eyes and saw the lovely face of Grace Devlin down the hall in room 360.

He had no business chasing after another woman so soon. That would be rebound unless it was just a cup of coffee. There was a restaurant downstairs. Maybe before dinner, just a cup of coffee, someone to spend time with, or maybe dinner. He could see how it went. Maybe on closer inspection, she might lose some of her mysterious tempting allure, maybe.

The restaurant was cozy and nearly empty. Grace felt a strange mixture of confusion and interest emanating from Ely Strickland, who sat rather close to her across the two-seater table. Outside, the marvelous view of the mountains was beginning to meld with the evening.

"So, what brought you here? I mean from—"

"Connecticut," she responded softly.

"Really? Wow, and you drove?"

She nodded, "I did. I really needed something completely different."

"I'm from New Orleans, pretty much the other side of the country."

"Long drive for you too."

He smiled. He had a bit of a dimple on the right side of his face, just the one. "Yeah, it was kind of planned for a while, percolating rather, a yen for the mountains."

"But we're not quite in the mountains. Are you going to keep going?"

He shrugged slightly, not really answering but continuing to look at her in that odd, searching way he'd done more than once since she'd met him here for coffee. "So, Grace, how about dinner?"

She smiled with amusement, "What about dinner?"

"Yeah, kind of unclear. Let me try again. Would you have dinner with me?"

She glanced away momentarily. It was all moving so fast. What was the plan here? She had no idea. "You seem, I don't know, preoccupied Ely. Are you sure this is a good idea?"

He looked down at his coffee cup, sort of swirling it around, making no effort to bring it back up to his lips. "Oh, probably not, but I'm still asking."

Then he brought those eyes up to her, so familiar, blue-gray, and something golden swirling deep within. "Okay, sure," she answered.

He smiled slowly, and she melted a little inside.

They headed to a quaint Italian restaurant just down the road from the hotel. It was closing on eight in the evening, and night had fallen into a sort of heavy shroud of darkness around them.

Strangely, it didn't feel foreboding to her but rather mysterious. Grace had always led a different sort of life. From the outside, one would call it extraordinary, but she didn't. It was quite normal for her, her normal.

"So, I haven't even asked if you're single. I mean, if you're married or seeing anyone."

She looked at him with a bit of surprise. There was no denying she lived significantly out of the mainstream. "No, I wouldn't have accepted your invitation if I was. I guess I'm a little old-fashioned about that kind of thing."

He smiled, "I didn't mean to be rude asking. I mean, these days, you well—"

She leisurely picked at her fettuccine. It was good, but she was nervous on so many levels. "And you?"

"No, I mean, there was someone, but that's over."

Without enough hesitation, she asked. "Is that what drove you to take this trip?"

He looked at her with curiosity. That was stupid. She had to be careful. He was feeling too much. "I-I don't know. I guess maybe in a tangential sort of way. The relationship, well, honestly, I'd felt a restlessness within it for a long time. I let it drag on, though, I'm not sure why. Look, I really didn't intend to talk about this."

"I don't mind," she murmured. He was confiding, and she felt that somehow it might be helpful.

"Yeah, well, it didn't end well. Jess felt very betrayed, upset, and made things ugly."

She sipped her wine, giving herself a moment to regroup. She could see things, images flashing across her mind as he spoke and could feel powerfully upsetting emotional confrontations as well. But that wasn't all that unusual when you were dealing with a drainer. They were addicted to the energy that they stole, and often the one losing energy was addicted to being drained as well. And most of the time, all of it took place on an unconscious level. It was a curious, messy, and damaging process. "Sorry, that couldn't have been easy."

"No, so yeah, sure getting away was very appealing. Trying to regain some perspective, sense of creativity again, all of that kind of felt drowned out—"

"In the uproar."

"Yes," his eyes brightened, recognizing that she understood what he was trying to say. "Exactly, in the uproar."

"So, there's really nobody lurking in your past, Grace?"

She glanced up, really liking the sound of her name on his lips but also feeling suddenly so oddly alien. How could she explain how she'd lived, conscious of things that most people never had a clue of, conscious of how fraught with complications and perils most romantic involvements were? Again, she sipped her wine, deciding to dodge the question. "Nothing recently. I guess I'm a workaholic of sorts."

Again, with the staring, he was definitely trying to figure her out. "You know, I've known a lot of workaholics. You don't strike me as that."

"Really, how do I strike you, Ely?"

"A little ethereal and oddly a little familiar."

"Grace, Gracie," her eyes opened. "Where are you, Gracie?"

She sat up in her room, in her white wrought iron daybed, peering into the semi-darkness. She'd heard a voice, but it didn't sound like a normal voice.

"I'm here," she whispered.

"What is here?" the voice asked softly.

She closed her eyes and allowed things to shift in the room ever so slightly by variables. And then she slowly reopened her eyes. There was a boy standing in the doorway, teenager, she thought, a good five to six years older than she.

"How did you get here?" she murmured.

"I don't know. I thought about you. Then I was here."

She looked around the shadowed room. Ah yes, clearly, she had traveled as well. It was different, decorated differently, with different furniture except for the bed. Her Mother had warned her about this possibility. "This isn't my place," she said.

"Are you sure?" he asked.

"Yep," she answered, laying back on a silky pink pillow that she suspected belonged to some other version of herself. Then she closed her eyes, willing herself back. She opened her eyes to her own bedroom. There was no teenage boy, teenage Ely, who had traveled to see her. Where she came from, he was no doubt quite different.

They drove back to the hotel in the darkness. Her family called them variables, all the different possibilities, existences that were possible for a spirit. Ever since she was a child, they had pounded that every experience in one's life was about learning, and most of those experiences were charted.

When she'd first arrived at the hotel, she made the mistake of traveling to one of those variable realities to seek Ely out initially. She'd been so rattled that she hadn't realized she'd done it unconsciously. That was why things were amiss, and there, his now ex-energy-drainer girlfriend was still in the picture.

He touched her hand, startling her out of her reflections. "Are you all right? You're so quiet."

"Sorry, tired, I suppose," she replied, more than a bit startled by the contact. This would be the first time he'd touched her.

He squeezed her hand — immediately electricity, attraction. This is what it feels like, she thought to herself. She'd never really experienced it before. She breathed in deeply, closing her eyes. She could feel a pull to him, waves of energy surrounding them both through their skin touching.

Perhaps it was unwise, but she opened herself to the shift, seeking, hoping for another plateau that was easier to deal with. This was not the same as accidentally shifting. This, in contrast, was quite deliberate. It was a peculiar feeling she remembered from long ago, requiring surrendering and letting go completely. It was no small feat to surrender to the universe and let a higher power take the reins of one's very existence, guiding her to where it was most helpful for her to be. But she'd learned to do it, and it had always yielded amazing things.

When she opened her eyes again, they were parked at the hotel. She glanced around. On first inspection, things looked the same. It was nighttime. Ely sat beside her silently. His hand was still on her arm as it had been when she decided to shift. But it was quiet, not like it had been before. That was the subtle difference. Everything around her felt enormously quiet. She glanced over to him in the semi-darkness and saw it immediately. Now he had a beard, before he'd been clean-shaven.

"Grace," he spoke, but she understood immediately the difference. He hadn't spoken aloud.

"Ely, how—" she began.

He squeezed her hand as he'd done before, but it was different this time. "No, Grace, not that way."

She leaned back in the seat, knowing instinctively what he meant. Focusing her energy on thought, she sent her words in a visual form to him. "I've changed."

"I can feel the difference. Why have you come here?"

She focused on the visuals. Pictures always travel faster than words. Her father had told her this. Her entire family was immersed in metaphysical training. This had always been her way of life. She focused on the draining and her confusion on how to help the other Ely recover from the blow he'd sustained.

The man next to her drew in a sharp breath. "I could feel that something was wrong, unstable. Let's go inside and figure out how to move forward."

Slight differences, slight shifts, the paintings on the walls, the décor in his hotel room, odd, there were two double beds, but in his room, there was more luggage for someone else.

She stared at it blankly. Could it be for the other one, for the blond woman?

"You're confused. She was only a passing acquaintance of mine." He continued to do it, speaking directly to her mind.

She stood up from sitting on the edge of one of the beds. "Please, can't we just speak? I'm not used to this."

He looked at her curiously, then spoke aloud. "Sorry, Grace. We've, well, the Grace I know, and I have been doing this for so long. It's become natural."

She nodded, "So, do you shift, I mean move to other variable plateaus as I do?"

He was sitting in the solitary desk chair, a beige one. The one in her room was black. "No, that's always been your gift."

Staring again at the obviously feminine piece of luggage, a deep burgundy tote bag. "Who are you—" then she stopped.

"You, Grace, we've been married for several years."

She took a sharp breath inward, of course, the differences, the variables. "Oh, where I'm from, we've just met. I mean, I think it's where I'm from. I lost track a bit at the beginning. I shifted accidentally, and saw you with the drainer, and I moved back into my frame where she wasn't around. There was some confusion," then she stopped. It all felt like such a muddle now.

"It's all right. I'm following."

She took a quick breath. "I just don't know what to do. For me, we just met. I don't know how to help."

He was staring intently at her as though it would be natural for him just to pull her into his arms. Yes, that would feel quite natural, but then it wasn't quite her that he would feel natural with. It was very confusing.

"It would be you, part of a greater you. As I am part of him, the one you've spent time with, and the other one — the one who is still with Jessica."

"So, you remember Jessica."

"Yes, I remember her. I knew what she was the moment I met her."

"So, why didn't he? The other you."

"It has to do with possibilities, variables as you've described. The entity encompassing all facets of me desires to learn. Thus all possibilities exist. Whatever choice was not made always exists somewhere."

"You're reading my mind. There are things I haven't said aloud."

There was a flicker of a smile. She decided she liked Ely with a beard, and she decided she liked Ely without a beard. "I'm sorry. Grace, my Grace, and I communicate nonverbally. There is always an exchange of thoughts. Our minds are wide open to each other."

"That sounds lovely," she murmured.

"It is," he said. Then he stood up and moved to her. "What you need is energy Grace, energy that only you and any version of me can create."

She began to question what he meant, but he'd pulled her into his arms and began kissing her. She thought to pull away, but the match had been lit. And she surrendered herself to the connection.

"We're here."

Her eyes snapped open. She was in the car again with Ely. But her cheeks flamed at the memory of the intimacy with the other Ely. "Are you all right, Grace?" he asked.

Her head was spinning. Things seemed the same here, and yet everything felt changed. It all bleeds over. She remembered.

She reached over and touched his bare arm. Deliberately, she poured the energy into him that she'd gained from her connection with the other Ely only moments before. He grabbed her hand with his own, held hers tightly, then leaned over and kissed her passionately. It wasn't the same as it had been with the other version of himself on that other plateau, but at the same time, it was very much the same.

Hotels in The Age of Covid

July 16th

Summer of 2020, a time that will live in infamy, possibly anyway.

Today is the day after 2020 taxes are due, delayed by several months because of the chaotic situation created by the Covid 19 pandemic. People everywhere are undoubtedly breathing a sigh of "What the hell!" Life seems poised on a precipice of uncertainty with this virus precariously straddling the wheel of fortune. Will things improve or just become more dire? As it is, anyone's guess will suffice.

I am living in the midst of it, researching an article or rather an opinion column on Hotels in the Age of Covid. Presently, I have just checked into an inn on Skyline Drive in the Blue Ridge Mountains.

The truth is that I haven't visited a hotel since before this pandemic began, in fact not since 2019. I write for the Richmond Times-Dispatch, currently from my little laptop computer. So, I must admit that I'm nervous. The world I once knew, felt so perhaps recklessly comfortable in, has seemed to have shifted overnight into something I don't recognize. We are living in a time of unknowns, uncertainty, and perhaps rampant indecision.

Mechanically, check-in at the Big Meadows Lodge was predominantly done online, and I just picked up my hotel key in the lobby. It's Friday afternoon, and I'm staying through Monday. The lobby was largely deserted except for a few hotel employees and the receptionist at the front desk stationed behind plexiglass, who gave me my key.

So, here's the strange new world with strange new rules. We all wear masks. People are somewhat faceless except for the top half, the eyes, and a muffled voice predominantly being the only mode of expression. It seems the days of sizing up people by their appearance are virtually out the window. Whether or not that's a good thing is up to history to decide.

I suppose it's safe to pronounce that we are in the middle of modern historical times, unprecedented times at any rate in many ways. However, many may justifiably argue that this is old territory retreaded citing examples of The Black Death, The Spanish Influenza, Yellow Fever, and countless other devastating outbreaks. What is certain is that the COVID-19 virus is highly contagious, and what we don't know about it far eclipses what we do.

But back to the task at hand.

The woman at the desk who checked me in was very friendly, in fact, one could say effusively so — to compensate, no doubt, for the "social distance" imposed by the virus. It is clear that people aren't sure exactly how to act just now. And in an odd respect, that's comforting. Because if people get too comfortable with this, then there is that possibility that hangs in the balance. The possibility that this is our world now, this antiseptic fearful terrain where no one touches, where—

The point would be how sad it would be if this indeed becomes the norm. In the present, we can only judge others by their behavior, less by appearance — an interesting side effect of the predicament we find ourselves in. So, behavior becomes more important and noticeable than before, perhaps.

She sighed deeply at the rough notes for her column. The real piece would no doubt be a different beast entirely. But she was ostensibly narrating, even these notes, to her unseen reader as most writers do, admittedly or not. She was on this, dare she say, strange adventure into an alien landscape virtually alone, her reader, listener, serving as her only companion. Her name was Bryce Seymour, and she was diving into the unknown.

Bryce: "Is it possible to find joy in this time? I mean, real joy during this life-altering pandemic?"

"That surely depends on what parameters you place on the definition of joy."

Bryce: "Joy, happiness, you know, the usual light fluttering feeling that puts a smile on your lips."

"That sounds easy, doesn't it? But if you place conditions on this feeling of joy. For example, security must be restored to the state I am familiar with for me to be happy — then you have a condition. If you must have nothing worrisome pending, then you have placed parameters on your happiness."

Bryce: "I see," she said aloud, though admittedly, she was still a little hazy.

"For real happiness, joy, you must disconnect it from the past, from worries of the future, anticipations. You must exist fully in the present, at this moment."

Bryce: "That seems difficult."

"Then it depends on how much you want it. Anything worthwhile comes with its challenges."

I settled into my exceptionally clean, quiet room. There would be no complimentary breakfast, only dining in the restaurant downstairs with masks and social distancing, or if you want to skip all that delightfulness, then room service.

There is no swimming in the pool outside, although it is the middle of summer, and no hanging out in groups without a mask and, of course, in small numbers.

Thank goodness there is still the breathtaking scenery surrounding the inn of the timeless Blue Ridge Mountains. It is comforting to have something near that at least appears unchanging.

These masks, the distancing, the limitations on social contact, and the tremendous economic impact and toll this pandemic is taking have been more than upsetting. It's been corrosively divisive. I know as I write, the world is battling with these restrictions, and within this country in particular. It is with a mixed heart that I witness this. On the one hand, I understand the impulse to resist that which changes your world from a familiar place to something that for some seems intolerable, but on the other hand, we all want to survive, not just individually but as a people. This virus connects us in an odd respect, all of us, depending on each of us to adhere to these new rules to stay alive. There is so much to discuss and explore here in depth.

For her now, however, the venue is this lovely hotel, rustic, but nothing particularly special about it except its location. She was here, alone, at this unparalleled time wondering how indeed one copes.

(Beginning again) Everything feels very antiseptic, as is the room. I can still smell the disinfectant which should be heartening but at this point, not so much, just a tad depressing.

So, she asked again, loudly to the universe. "How does one achieve joy in the era of COVID-19?" especially if you're alone.

"Are you feeling alone?"

Bryce: She considered the question. "Yes, I suppose I am, particularly now. I never used to feel that way in hotels. I like them, or rather liked them, the way they used to be. But now it just feels scary, as though the ground isn't solid beneath my feet, uncertain, intimidating."

"It's a scary time — far afield from what is familiar, expected, comfortable."

Bryce: "Yes, the unknown is a scary place to perch."

Now, more than at other times, she did wish she had someone. It wasn't as if she was going to meet anyone new right now under these conditions.

There seemed to be a beat.

What was she doing? One might wonder, might ask. She didn't blame them for being curious. It is a curious thing. No, she didn't have multiple personalities. It's automatic writing, actually. She'd been doing it for ages, in fact, since she was a kid.

The process itself is quite simple. Place your pen/pencil on the paper, holding your hand that grips it still. Clear your mind, and let it write, yes, by itself.

The first time she tried it, she was spurred on by an old spooky movie where a psychic contacted the great beyond through automatic writing. Of course, when it actually worked for her, she thought she was talking to herself. Then it became clear that was not the case.

"You were 13."

Bryce: "That's right. You remember."

She'd always written in journals, but this unique connection started out of the blue. As she said, she thought it was her at first, but —

"It wasn't. I am a separate consciousness."

Bryce: "A guide of sorts."
"At times, I call myself Julian."

Julian, her contact, how could she explain what this is about? At times, the connection, communication rather, feels shaky, insubstantial, and at other times as though they were in the same room together, just speaking to each other.

A guide? Yes, and sometimes just a friend. When her father died, Julian guided her through the grief and helped her to see the reality that life continues. It gave her strength, but a change of perspective can often be positive. Perhaps that is truly what is needed in these challenging times, a change of perspective.

Anyway, back to her and the lack of a relationship. She was 33, and she'd never been married. Close once, but something held her back. His name was Brandon. They'd been seeing each other for about six months, but when he asked her to marry him, well, she choked. She actually felt cold all over, chills, really, so she said no. He worked at the newspaper, never spoke to her again, and eventually moved on to another job.

"Your spirit intervened. The relationship would have been very damaging for you."

Bryce: "My spirit? That sounds like something separate from me."

"Yes and no, the spirit is the eternal part of you which lives through many incarnations on earth and elsewhere, often simultaneously."

"Simultaneously?"

"Yes, the goal is to evolve, to learn through whatever means. What you perceive as your life on earth is not at all what you believe it to be — its purpose or reality."

She took a breath and considered, allowing all that to soak in. She thought again about her father.

"Yes, of course, your father George's life did not simply cease to exist because his flesh perished. His spirit, his essence, moved onto another kind of existence. In fact, he is often near you whenever he is in your reflections."

She stilled herself and considered what Julian was telling her and that he'd once again picked up on her thoughts before she voiced them. It was undeniable that she felt her father near her at times and was surprised when she turned around, and he was not standing there. And then there were the dreams as well.

"Dreams are not at all what your culture purports them to be. They are your consciousness opening to other realities that your spirit exists within, other dimensions, plateaus of existence. Your conception of this world, this finite world that you have trained your perception to accept, is truly an illusion. You are not nearly as trapped as you believe yourselves to be."

Bryce: "Trapped but trapped is what everyone feels, particularly in the midst of this virus."

"Creation is vast, Bryce, amazingly vast, and no one is trapped."

The first night in the hotel, she did dream. She dreamed of Julian. He appeared as a tall, dark-haired man wearing a simple cotton, white button-down shirt over blue jeans, which was pretty ordinary for a spirit guide.

She felt somewhat amazed when she saw him because she knew him instantly though she'd never seen him before as an actual person. "What's wrong, Bryce?" he asked a little somberly.

"It's silly," she said. "I didn't expect you to be so casual."

He didn't smile back at her, though she felt warmth from him. "I like to be comfortable."

They were still in the hotel, though it felt remarkably altered and disconnected from what she remembered of it. She was dressed in a long gypsy floral broomstick skirt that she had shoved in her suitcase but not worn yet, and a long black top over it. "What are we doing?" she murmured.

"Spending time together," he answered, not elaborating much. That was odd for him. She usually couldn't stop him from elaborating.

Then, he did smile. She found it unexpected, though she liked his smile. But she suspected he usually maintained a more stoic expression with his sharp cheekbones and intensely focused dark eyes, quite handsome, she had to admit.

"I'm not always dour," he murmured as they continued to walk down the hallway. It was markedly filled with light and much larger than usual. "This is how I see your environment," he commented.

"Really, so different?"

"Everyone experiences the same reality differently as everyone has quite a hand in creating their own reality."

She wasn't sure she'd heard him correctly. "Creating? I don't understand."

"What you experience, you are also the creator of. Everyone lives a very personalized version of their existence. Consider different witnesses to an event, all of them describing varied interpretations of the same thing, often markedly different."

"I-I'm not sure—" Seems she had trouble wrapping her brain around the idea.

"It's all right. Mull it over. It will make sense at some point. Everything has its own time," he explained. His voice was deep but comforting and oddly familiar to her. She knew that whenever they spoke to each other through the writing in the future, she would now hear this voice.

She stopped at a large picture window at the end of the hall. Outside, the weather seemed turbulent, stormy, and the mountains were tremendous and very close, not as she remembered outside the hotel. "That is different. Why so turbulent?"

"Collective energy, people are confused and upset right now. The storm is just a reflection of that chaotic energy."

She stared at it, feeling it tangibly on her skin — irritation, panic.

"Step back," he murmured, putting his hand on her shoulder. She could feel it, a warmth emanating from his touch, passing right into her, calming her.

"Why are you here?" she whispered.

"I didn't want you to feel alone."

"Will we ever meet? I mean, outside of dreams?"

"One day, when you reach where I exist, but don't worry. I'll always be near you, like your father."

She supposed she should have been upset at that. They'd never meet, not really in the flesh in this lifetime. But she wasn't. She felt a peacefulness within as though she'd evolved a bit, not nearly attached to that physical world in the same way she'd been before, and as a result, not nearly so frightened of her vulnerability.

Julian's words, "No one is trapped." She took some time to consider them in the light of that extraordinary dream from the night before and what was happening around her. It is odd if one thinks about it a bit differently. This time of Covid-19 was, in many ways, a period of forced reflection for people. Usual exterior entertainments have been curtailed — large gatherings, plays, movies, concerts, parties, and all the external activities that fill our lives with pleasant distractions, so to speak. So, what does that leave us? More time indeed for thinking, personal reflection, and going internal for life's meaning instead of outward.

"No one is trapped."

That would definitely be a hard sell for some. But if it's all true. If we are not flesh but spirit, and this world is just a small piece of our "real" stomping grounds, then what does that mean? What does it mean about the real purpose of living and where we all place our priorities?

She wandered the halls of the hotel, alone this time. But she looked with new eyes, examining everything differently as though trying to see it for the first time without past judgments. It didn't bother her in the same way, the emptiness and quiet that had so intimidated her at first. It felt oddly full, as though just beyond a door, beyond a wall, there was a newness that she had yet to see.

"How is the column coming?"

Bryce: She remembered him from the night before. Now she could see him quite concretely in her mind. "Slow, I'm afraid I've been pulled off-track."

"You mean because of what we've discussed."

Bryce: "Yes, it feels as though my mind is exploding with new information."

"Maybe that's a good thing. Maybe it's good to find a new perspective for what you're writing."

Bryce: "I suppose, but I'm unsure what my angle is now. Originally, it was just how much things have changed during the pandemic, more narrowly hotels."

"Yes, but Bryce, there could be a whole universe inside this small hotel. Can you see that?"

Bryce: "Stop it. I'm confused enough."

"Then allow things to settle before you begin again."

She took a long walk in the early morning. That was when things were most deserted, well, even more deserted anyway. In the time of Covid, you had to consider how to avoid people. Of course, the mask was always with her. The way she would carry her wallet, her driver's license, she must now carry her mask.

Some don't wear it outside. But there is some mixed messaging and confusion about whether it might be necessary, so she brought it and wore it. Was she worried about getting sick?

That is a question. She believed the fear was largely of the unknown. Some people become ill but mildly with no incident, and others, well, others become quite ill, and some die.

She wondered what the purpose of the unknown was. What was the purpose of tearing us forcibly out of our comfort zone?

It forces us to acknowledge that we are not in control.

We cannot exert personal control over the unknown. Is that where faith comes in? Trust, belief, and hope, she supposed. All were essential things that modern culture has often spent time disavowing.

But the question then becomes, can we have faith and hope if we actively deny it to others?

Are we truly in this together?

Bryce: "How connected are we all?"

Some days she could anticipate him, anticipate his answers before they were written, but not today. Today he was more distant.

"That is surely the crux of things. Isn't it, Bryce?"

She waited, having virtually no idea where he was going with this.

Bryce: "The crux?"

"There are laws, spiritual consequences of cause and effect."

Bryce: "Are you speaking of karma?"

"Karma is not what it is believed to be. It is not a punishment meted out for wrongdoing. There is not a construction of judgment anywhere but in your self-created physical world. It is a faulty, fallible construction. There is no right or wrong. There is, however, choice and its consequences. Do you choose what produces negative consequences, negative ramifications, and negative energy, or do you choose what produces growth and positive consequences? And learning can actually be achieved in either arena."

Bryce: "I see. I think." But she wasn't really sure that she did. From an incredibly young age, people were actively groomed in the notions of right and wrong and judgment — a whole lot of judgment about everything and everybody.

"So, as there are always consequences, for you to reject your fellow human being, judge them, and make choices that affect them for ill, you must be ready to accept the consequences. Everyone is free to choose. It is your divine right, your free will, but you are not free from the consequences of that choice."

Bryce: "And with this virus, we depend on each other. In fact, we could be responsible for making each other ill. Surely, there is a lesson in that."

"Yes, when we cannot seem to absorb a lesson subtly, the universe hoists a heftier presentation of that lesson upon us. Everyone must learn. No matter how long it takes, we will learn."

So, these conversations with Julian, which often involved severe cramping in her hand as she was writing so quickly, simultaneously opened her mind to new considerations and confused her greatly. What was her role in all of this?

This was an aspect that she couldn't fail to consider. She wrote for a newspaper that had a substantial circulation. In a nutshell, people read her stuff. But if she started droning on about spiritual lessons, karma, and evolving, then not only would people probably not listen, but she might very well lose her job.

So, what, indeed, was her purpose in all of this?

How could she impart what she was learning, understanding, and not alienate her readers?

"As you say, you do have to consider your audience. As I speak to you, I consider how I can impart a truth in a way that you will most easily absorb."

Bryce: "What does that mean that you're dumbing this stuff down for me?"

There was a hesitation. She could feel him considering.

"You know. I didn't mean that, Bryce."

Bryce: She knew that. He would never, well, she knew he would never do that. "Yes, of course, I know. I'm just feeling frustrated."

"If I were to converse with you in ancient Greek, it would be useless to you. You must speak the language of your audience. Baby steps, Bryce — what does your audience need?"

Bryce: "Need? What do they need? Reassurance, I suppose, and maybe a hopeful way to navigate this."

"Yes, perhaps without being overt, you can slowly navigate them to that end to the true purpose of this time, this time of learning."

Bryce: "Ah, I think I see what you mean." Perhaps that was it, not a cold hard look at what we've lost, but how to find meaning and purpose in the present. What can we learn about ourselves, about our world, during this time on the edge?

I can't help but think about Charles Dickens' famous quote from A Tale of Two Cities, "It was the best of times. It was the worst of times." No doubt, and with good reason, most would consider the latter to be true. But there is always the possibility of duality in every experience, every time. Is there something positive that we can pull from this very difficult period? Is there potential for growth here within the human spirit? Perhaps, instead of resisting, a moment should be taken. Perhaps, each of us should take that private moment to truly evaluate what is important. Perhaps the truth is, although we might resist it, that we are indeed our brother's keeper. Of course, not in a judgmental way, but in a basic sense, we do bear responsibility tangentially for each other's well-being. Just in acknowledging the spread of this virus and how we need to work to keep each other safe, we are each other's keepers. And perhaps instead of that being a burden, we might consider what a great privilege that it can be. A gift to others and ourselves as well.

Bryce: "Is that what you mean?"

"It is a beginning, Bryce Seymour. A very promising beginning."

More Books by Evelyn Klebert

The Tethering: A Portent of Crows

6 x 9 Softcover 190 pages

ISBN 978-1613425992

Deborah Brandt's beloved Aunt Gena always told her that she was special, a bit different, and would have to live her life unlike other people. Of course, this she disregarded as the ramblings of her lovely but notably eccentric aunt. Although there were the things that Aunt Gena said that seemed true — like Deborah being sensitive to energy shifts, having potentially psychic impressions, and dreaming of a spirit guide — none of it could be real. But the most ridiculous thing that her Aunt Gena told her before she died is that there is someone special out there for her. She said that he is an extraordinary man who is not only her perfect match but someone who she would learn from so that they could help the world in difficult times. How ridiculous! It sounds like a fairy tale, and no such person exists.

Daniel Wren is unique. He has been raised and trained from a young age to hone his psychic gifts. He lives in a world unimagined by most. And he has been waiting for years to contact his counterpart, soulmate if you will. But the problem is that she is painfully unaware of the type of life that he lives and the life she would be entering into if they came together.

His dilemma becomes how best to proceed. How can he win her over and move forward before outside forces take that decision away from him?

Gravier's Bookshop

A New Orleans Paranormal Mystery (#1)

6 x 9 Softcover 190 pages

ISBN 978-1-61342-288-5

Max Gravier had no intention of becoming a recluse, but after his wife's death it seems his life is heading in that direction. He spends his time running Gravier's Bookshop on Magazine Street and occasionally on the quiet helps the police solve a crime with his psychic sensitivities. That is until he answers Caroline's call, a cry for help, out of his dreams that draws him into a fierce battle for a young woman's soul.

In this first installment of The New Orleans Paranormal Mystery series, Caroline Breslin, an amazingly gifted empath, is determined to strike out on her own and has moved out from the protection of her family home. All is going extremely well until of course she comes under siege from a devastating supernatural attack. The last thing Caroline wants is to run back to her family for help, even though she is painfully in over her head. What she really needs is a knight in shining armor or maybe just that guy that keeps haunting her dreams.

The Hotel Mandolin (#2)

A New Orleans Paranormal Mystery

6 x 9 Softcover 138 pages

ISBN 978-1-61342-290-8

Peril is wrapped up in the most enticing of disguises, in *The Hotel Mandolin,* the second installment of The New Orleans Paranormal Mystery series. It's opulent, it's classic, and it's one of the most renowned hotels nestled deep in New Orleans' famous business district, but something is amiss at The Hotel Mandolin. PI Peter Norfleet is calling out the big guns to help him investigate a recent suicide at the famous establishment — his good friend Max Gravier, a formidable psychic, and his girlfriend Caroline Breslin, a talented empath. But none of them can seem to scratch the surface of this puzzle, no one except Cassie Breslin, Caroline's clairvoyant mother, who has somehow tapped into an unexpected connection with a tragic ghost from the turn of the century. And the more she uncovers the more dangerous and malevolent the mystery becomes.

The House at Pritchard Place (#3)

A New Orleans Paranormal Mystery

6 x 9 Softcover 170 pages

ISBN 978-1-61342-292-2

Nothing is really wrong with the old Warrick House on Dante St. except that there most certainly is. Nothing is exactly wrong with its new mysterious owner except that Elise is sure that something doesn't add up. In the third installment of The New Orleans Paranormal Mystery series, with the help of the very psychic Breslin clan, Elise is about to embark on a wild rescue mission into another dimension that will land her squarely somewhere she doesn't expect, right back into her past. Right back to a childhood home whose memory still haunts her to this day -- *The House at Pritchard Place.*

Dragonflies - Journeys into the Paranormal

6 x 9 Softcover 120 pages

ISBN 978-1-88756-072-6

A powerful wizard, love-crossed ghosts, a mysterious dark warrior, and an enigmatic time traveler -- a mystical wordsmith entices you into the world of the paranormal with a collection of inspired stories. Each tale takes the journey of the dragonfly imbued with the momentum and energy of change, following a winding path that ultimately will lead you to find the truth buried beneath perception.

Treading on Borrowed Time

6 x 9 Softcover 198 pages

ISBN 978-1-61342-214-4

For Julia Moreau life seems complicated. Emerging from a failed marriage and managing a lifetime of diabetes, she lives alone in her childhood home where she communicates with the spirit of her Great Aunt Lilia. But Julia doesn't have a clue what complicated is until she is thrust into being the key chess piece in a match between two powerful men of extraordinary abilities on the wild hunt for a mystical creature hidden in the heart of New Orleans' French Quarter. Will Julia lose her soul to the karma of a devastating past life or her heart to the love of a man driven by dark forces? What is clear is that whichever way she turns she is *Treading on Borrowed Time.*

The Lady in the Blue Dress

6 x 9 Softcover 214 pages

ISBN 978-1088106891

When she was a child, Mika Devalieur was introduced to her grandmother's most precious possession - a priceless and mysterious painting that she simply called The Lady in the Blue Dress. Upon Adele St. Clair's death, the painting is left in the care of her granddaughter with only one stipulation. Mika must hand over the family heirloom to a total stranger. Mika Devalieur desperately wants to deny her beloved grandmother's last request, but she can't. Torn between her Gran's last wishes and her desire to hold onto the Lady, she ultimately journeys to rural Virginia, where an enigmatic man shows her that this painting is only the beginning.

What quickly becomes clear is that James Clairmont knows much more about her and the Lady than he is letting on. He begins to slowly unravel a powerful supernatural connection that spans three generations of her family. Mika finds herself desperate to uncover the entire truth before she falls in love with a man filled with so many secrets - secrets about him, about her, and most especially about The Lady in the Blue Dress.

A Quiet Moment

6 x 9 Softcover 295 pages

ISBN 978-1-61342-326-4

Jacob Wyss is caught in a rut, in fact on the verge of being engulfed by it. After an excruciating and disillusioning divorce, his life as an artist in a sleepy-college town at the foot of the Appalachian Mountains has become quiet, routine, and maddening in its predictability. One wintry day, his deep restlessness drives him out in precarious conditions to a largely empty bookstore nearly devoid of another living soul, nearly.

Aimee Marston isn't like everyone else. On the surface, she lives a sedate life working as a feature writer for a small local newspaper in addition to several other editorial jobs to help make ends meet. But just beneath, her existence is largely not her own. She is a sensitive, an empathetic psychic, guided by her calling to use her gifts to help others. Unfortunately, as a result, her secretiveness has made her defensive, protective of herself, and prevented her from having much of a life of her own.

A psychic call for help sends Aimee out on a freezing January morning where her destiny and Jacob's collide sending both their lives spiraling onto an unexpected and often disturbing track. Two lonely souls connect, not by accident, but by design. Theirs is the intersection of two spiritual paths, two lovers who must struggle to overcome the phantoms of a past life, as well as the challenges of their own inner demons to carve out an extraordinary future together.

Travels into the Breach - Accounts of a Reclusive Mystic

6 x 9 Softcover 176 pages

ISBN 978-1-61342-323-3

At first glance, his life seems quiet, serene, and even uneventful. Malachi McKellan, a 65 five-year-old widower and author of esoteric books, lives largely as a recluse in a house situated just off the banks of Bayou St. John in New Orleans. But unbeknownst to most, he is also a bit of a detective, a specific kind of detective whose specialty is psychic attacks. Alongside his lifelong companion and spirit guide Simon Tull, a nineteenth century, twenty something English gent, Malachi battles the unseen, and is an unacknowledged hero to the most vulnerable - most of the population who have no idea what is really happening beneath the surface of the world in which they live.

In this collection of adventures, Malachi McKellan and Simon Tull wage war against the most insidious elements of the paranormal. In "The Three," Malachi and Simon come to the aid of a young woman being victimized by a group of dark witches. An old apartment building is the scene of an unimaginable battle against monstrous forces in "The Lost Soul." Malachi and Simon find themselves strategizing against a psychic vampire in "Obsession," and "The Hotel" turns back time to the 1980's where Malachi confronts a demonic spirit. In "Between," a past life is revisited as Malachi attempts to rescue a beloved sister from committing her existence to vengeance, and "The Wedding" takes a personal turn when Malachi must confront painful truths while endeavoring to protect his niece from a potentially devastating union. Travel into the Breach with a pair of paranormal warriors who choose to confront overwhelming forces on a battlefield unsuspected by most.

A Ghost of a Chance

6 x 9 Softcover 174 pages

ISBN 978-1-88756-050-4

Jack Brennan, an ambitious high-powered attorney dies, only to find himself constrained to a peculiar afterlife as an earth-bound spirit trapped in an old Virginia farmhouse with a very much living, reclusive writer of campy vampire novels. Hallie Barkly recovering from a painful and disillusioning divorce has forged a career and exorcised her demons by writing under the pseudonym of Sebastian Winters. Their lives intersect, and two unconventional lovers are brought together under insurmountable circumstances. They must battle an unseen force hell-bent on possessing Hallie's life and bridge death itself to make possible what cannot be - to find a chance.

Explanations

6 x 9 Softcover 82 pages

ISBN 978-1-93493-515-6

In this, her second poetry collection, Evelyn Klebert takes us down the intricate path of a personal journey. Life with its particular struggles, pit- falls, and ultimately triumphs clearly begins to mirror a universal path, the quest for answers that we all ultimately pursue. In this reflective, esoteric collection we can all explore and seek some of life's elemental mysteries and hopefully when all is said and done emerge with some *Explanations.*

Sanctuary of Echoes

6 x 9 Softcover 338 pages

ISBN 978-1-61342-211-3

Corey Knight was more than convinced that all she could look forward to now was a quiet, reclusive life spent living out the rest of her days in her childhood home on the fringes of New Orleans' French Quarter. But the unexpected specter of her deceased father plunges her into a mad quest for a missing supernatural weapon unearthed long ago. And unfortunately, her only ally is a lost love who she betrayed.

Iain Shaw returns to New Orleans, a city he abandoned a decade before while fleeing a devastating past. Here, he is only confronted by it again in the visage of the woman he once adored — the one he is now determined to get back at any cost.
Follow them both in a wild supernatural tale of discovery and redemption as they confront and unearth the echoes of a buried and unyielding truth that once tore them irreparably apart.

Breaking Through the Pale

6 x 9 Softcover 92 pages

ISBN 978-1-88756-045-0

Breaking Through the Pale is a compelling collection of paranormal short stories by metaphysical author Evelyn Klebert.

"Contact" is the tale of a woman who life is irrevocably altered when she unexpectedly establishes communication with a spiritual guide.

In "A Grey Mourning," a disillusioned man encounters a mysterious being on the foggy streets of New Orleans.

"Dancing on the Threshold" relates the story of a woman who precariously poised between life and death takes a journey that unravels the true nature of her life.

"Isolation" is the story of a woman who inexplicably finds herself alone and disoriented in an old, quaint house on the edge of a forest. Slowly, she must piece together the past that brought her to this place and the mystical implications surrounding her predicament.

The Witches' Own

6 x 9 Softcover 124 pages

ISBN 978-1-61342-058-4

On the surface things seem quiet and serene in the picturesque coastal village of Kilmarnock, Virginia. But something unseen roams its lush forests as the past and present collide and the unthinkable begins to wreak its vengeance. Young Lucy Bonner is executed for witchcraft in the town's distant and brutal past. Her death triggers an unholy chain of events which grasp at the restless heart of novelist Peter McQuade, spurring him towards a quest to uncover the dark and terrifying truth.

The Broken Vow

Vol. I of The Clandestine Exploits of a Werewolf

6 x 9 Softcover 140 pages

ISBN 978-1-61342-133-8

In the heart of every man, there is a history. In the heart of every monster, there is a story. In this first installment of *The Clandestine Exploits of a Werewolf,* Ethan Garraint is on a vendetta that begins in the heart of the Pyrenees with the fall of Montségur and leads him to the streets of New Orleans nearly five hundred years later. But the person he chases isn't really a man anymore and Ethan has been a werewolf for almost a millennium. With the aid of a gifted seer, he is on a blood hunt that will culminate in a journey that crosses the line between heaven and earth and ends somewhere in between.

The Left Palm

And Other Halloween Tales of the Supernatural

6 x 9 Softcover 104 pages

ISBN 978-1-93493-556-9

Just when all seems well and quiet when all becomes comfortable and predictable then reality bends. Evelyn Klebert takes you to a place where ordinary life fractures into the sphere of the paranormal.

The journey begins with one woman's unstoppable quest for vengeance against a supernatural creature in "Wolves," and continues in an old historical graveyard where a horrifying discovery is uncovered in "Emma Fallon." In "The Soul Shredder" a psychiatrist's unusual patient opens his eyes to a disturbing new view of reality, while in "Wildflowers" a woman strikes up a supernatural friendship with impossible implications. And in "The Left Palm" a fortuneteller in the French Quarter receives a most unexpected and terrifying customer.

Considerations

6 x 9 Softcover 68 pages

ISBN 978-1-88756-062-7

Sometimes the struggle to understand the meaning and complexities of living comes down to a single moment of introspection or a fleeting yet meaningful reflection. This collection of poetry by Evelyn Klebert takes you down a winding path of self-discovery where the resolution may not always be absolute, but the journey is indeed unforgettable. It a wide and varied map of inspired poetry for your examination and consideration.

Visit Evelyn's website at:

www.evelynklebert.com

Cornerstone Book Publishers
www.cornerstonepublishers.com